Peter u_____ *wr*

*that the house was haunted. Jan
wanted to run out of the room, but
she was afraid . . . the constant
groanings and creakings of doors
and floor boards had made all six
Bradys sit up . . . they waited, in
suspense, to see if the pirate ghosts
would appear . . .*

Greg was especially impressed
with the girl, a slim, pretty creature who was the most beautiful
young person he had seen in a
long time.

Harker's smile was grim as he
looked at Cindy and Bobby. "Like I
said, Mathews, we've got to get rid of
the evidence!"

Other TIGER BEAT Books
You'll Want to Read

The Brady Bunch

in

"The Treasure of Mystery Island"

by
JACK MATCHA

AN OFFICIAL TIGER BEAT PUBLICATION

Distributed by The New American Library, Inc.,
1301 Avenue of the Americas, New York, New York 10019

Cover design by Bill Cragun

FOURTH PRINTING
FIFTH PRINTING
SIXTH PRINTING
SEVENTH PRINTING
EIGHTH PRINTING
NINTH PRINTING
TENTH PRINTING
ELEVENTH PRINTING
TWELFTH PRINTING

FIRST PRINTING, OCTOBER, 1972

CHAPTER ONE

The trip to Mystery Island was thought up during a breakfast conversation one Sunday in May. It began casually, almost out of the blue. It was a hot, muggy, sunshine-filled day and everybody around the table was feeling kind of lazy.

"Gee, I wish it were vacation time already," Peter said, yawning. "It feels too hot to even move. I'd love to jump into a pool or something. Hey, Dad, where are we going this summer?"

Almost at once like a lighted fuse the kids all began to talk about where they'd like to go. Greg, who loved surfing, wanted to go to a good beach with big waves. Someone else mentioned the mountains and a third mentioned a nice lake they'd been to years earlier. But Greg was too excited about surfing and turned to his mother for support.

Carol Brady sighed as she looked at her smiling husband, Mike, and grinned at the six young faces eyeing her watchfully.

"It's up to your father," she said.

At once six heads turned eagerly in his direction. Mr. Brady, who had been checking through his mail, frowned slightly and held up a letter he had just finished reading.

"How about going to an island this year?" he asked casually.

"An island?" Peter repeated. "An island where? You mean in one of the lakes we've gone to?"

"That sounds dull," Marcia said wrinkling up her nose. "They're so tiny—those islands—you practically fall off if you walk two blocks."

"Not this one," Mr. Brady said. "This one's pretty big. Several miles wide, in fact. And it isn't in a lake. It's in the ocean just off the coast of Maine."

"An island off the coast of Maine!" Jan exclaimed, her eyes widening with new interest. "What's it called?"

"Mystery Island," Mr. Brady said.

The name caused a flurry of excitement. The kids looked at one another and wanted to know all about it. How big was it, how far was it from the coastline. Above all, how it got that name?

Mr. Brady smiled understandingly at their excitement. They had never gone to an island in the ocean and they had never been to New England.

"Does it have pirates?" Jan asked quickly. "It must have with a name like that."

"How about buried treasure?" Bobby cried.

Cindy wanted to know if it had wild animals as well.

"What's it like Daddy?" little Cindy asked, her eyes as big as saucers.

"I'll look it up in the big atlas inside," Greg said suddenly and scraped back his chair.

"You'll be wasting your time," Mr. Brady said, laughing. "It's too small to be in there."

He looked at the faces confronting him, then at his pretty blond wife and winked at her. "You think we ought to keep Mystery Island a mystery till we get there, Carol?" he asked wistfully.

"Oh, no, darling," she grimaced. "Don't keep them in suspense that long. They won't be able to sleep now you've mentioned it."

"Neither will I," a voice behind them chimed in irritably. They turned to see Alice carrying a tray loaded with freshly-baked rolls. "Tell us now Mr. Brady please. I'm dying of suspense."

Mike Brady laughed. "Well there's nothing like working up a good audience. Okay, I'll tell you all about it. Mystery Island isn't very big. It's a speck of land really. Just a few miles in each direction from the center. But it's beautiful. Full of great beaches and some good hills to climb if you feel like it.

"It's about an hour off the coast of Maine by ferry and it's settled mostly by fishing families, though there did used to be a kind of pirates' colony there in the seventeenth century."

"Pirates!" the Brady kids yelled in unison. Mike Brady grinned, having known exactly how they would react when he tossed out the word "Pirate."

"Yep, pirates. 'Yo-ho-ho and a bottle of rum,' " Mr. Brady said. "You see the island's sort of out of the way. It has a good natural harbor and plenty of caves to hide loot in. According to what I heard, several of the biggest pirates sailing in that time used the island at one time or another."

"Are they still there, Daddy?" Bobby asked carefully.

"Is it dangerous?" Jan asked worriedly.

"Well, I don't think so really, children," Mr. Brady said. "It's been a long time since the place was used by freebooters. But I must tell you that the caves are still supposed to be haunted by the pirates' ghosts!"

"Darling, tell them *why* we are going there," Carol said.

Mike Brady pulled a letter from his inside pocket. "Well that's simple enough to explain. One of my clients, Matt Arnold, who owns about ten factories, was very happy with a building I designed for him and offered me a kind of bonus—the bonus being a free vacation to his place on Mystery Island. He's got a lovely cottage there. He usually goes down there summers to fish and swim and do a little boating, but this year he's got to stay here. Too many factory problems. So he asked us," Mr. Brady concluded with a smile. "We leave as soon as school's over."

"How long does it take to drive there?" Marcia asked, her eyes shining.

8

"We're not going by car," Mr. Brady said. "That's part of the vacation. We'll all be flown to Maine!"

"In a plane?" Cindy asked.

"How else?" Mr. Brady asked gently, patting his ten-year-old daughter's head. "Mr. Arnold's putting the company plane at our disposal. Soon as we're ready to go, we just call the office. They'll follow through."

"How long will it take?" Bobby wanted to know.

"Can I take my dolls?" Cindy asked.

"What do you want to take your silly old dolls on a vacation to an island for?" Peter said scornfully.

"How big are the caves?" Jan asked.

The questions began to fly at Mr. Brady so thick and fast that he held up one hand.

"Whoa! I'm not finished with breakfast yet. I just gave you a whole bunch of information. The rest of it will have to wait till this afternoon. I'll be glad to set up an information booth in the den at that time."

"Can I ask just one more now?" Bobby asked a little timidly because he saw his father looking anxiously at the fresh rolls that were fast growing cold on the table.

"Go ahead, Bobby," Mr. Brady said gently.

"Are there any wild animals on the island? Like lions or tigers?"

Greg and Marcia laughed at the question.

"They don't have tigers in Maine," Greg said. "Just ghosts!"

"Big ghosts?" Cindy asked worriedly.

"I don't think so, Cindy," Mr. Brady said reassuringly. "I really shouldn't have mentioned the ghosts. It's probably just one of those things they've invented for the tourist trade." He looked about quickly as if he were eager to change the subject.

"Any other questions before I finish my breakfast?"

Alice came forward and grinned. "Are there any good looking fishermen on the island? And I don't mean ghosts, either."

Everybody laughed at that. Alice had just about given up hoping that her boyfriend Sam would marry her. The good-natured butcher seemed to evade the question whenever it came up.

"I don't know what we'll find on Mystery Island," Mr. Brady said, eyes twinkling. "Want us to take Sam along?" he said jokingly.

"Not on your life," Alice snorted. "If I find a good-looking man on the island, it'll just be Sam's tough luck."

The conversation about Mystery Island ended there, but that wasn't really the end of it. For the next few weeks, the island was in their thoughts almost constantly. Greg and Marcia went to the library and learned that the island had been settled in 1672 and that there had indeed been a nest of pirates, among them a big red-bearded giant by the name of Red Andrew who had hidden away shipments of gold he had stolen from ships of the Spanish fleet that sailed to Spain from South America.

Red Andrew had had an enemy named Black

Tom, an Irish pirate, who challenged his foes to duels and then poisoned the tip of his sword with a special poison invented by Indians in the Caribbean Sea. In 1698 there had been a big fight between the two pirate leaders for possession of Mystery Island as a base. Red Andrew had accused Black Tom of cheating him at cards and had told him bluntly he was unwelcome. He and his men could no longer share the island with them.

According to the book that Greg and Marcia had read to the other kids, Black Tom had immediately challenged Red Andrew to a duel. The entire crews of the pirate ships had gathered around the battlers. As they set up a huge, resounding chant, the two pirate chiefs slashed at one another with swords. As usual, Black Tom's sword was poisoned at the tip. But Red Andrew, a shrewd fellow, had learned of his trick and was prepared. He made sure that Tom drank more than he did just before the fight began.

Then, when the fight was underway, he arranged to drop to one knee as if he were falling. Black Tom was taken by surprise as Andrew, whom he thought was ill or hurt, suddenly struck his sword and knocked it out of his hand. Before he could get the weapon back, Red Andrew seized it and stabbed him in the arm with it. In a few moments the deadly Indian poison had killed Black Tom.

"According to the legend," Greg said in a low voice, "the ghost of Black Tom stalks through the island in search of revenge against any kin of Red Andrew who might be foolish enough to visit it."

"You mean anybody who was related to him at all?" asked Jan incredulously.

"Of course," Greg said.

"Well, how does anyone know if he is a part of that family?" Peter asked. "I mean you could be a second cousin twice removed and maybe your great, great, great, great grandfather was Red Andrew. You mean Black Tom's ghost would still chase after you?"

"That's right," Greg said. "Better hope we aren't related to old Andrew. We might never get back!"

He and Marcia smiled and promptly forgot it. But the youngest Bradys didn't and especially not Cindy and Bobby. They found it a little too much to go to sleep with.

About an hour past their bedtime, both children began to worry about the shadows thrown on the ceiling by the moonlight across the leaves outside their window. Without a word they lay there looking anxiously at the moving figures.

After a while Cindy got frightened. The figure looked very much like a ghost to her. Was it possible, she wondered, that Black Tom had heard Greg read them the legend and was angry? So angry that he was haunting their bedroom?

Bobby was worried, too, but about something else. He wondered seriously if the Bradys were part of the pirate's family. Maybe Red

12

Andrew had been his great, great, great, great, great cousin or uncle or something like that.

Shortly afterward, Cindy got out of her bed and tiptoed to her parents' bedroom. Silently, she crept beneath the sheets and moved close to her mother.

A few minutes later, Bobby found it too scary to sleep too and got up. He walked quietly into his parents' room and snuggled in close to his mother. The shadows in the room were moving on the ceiling. But this time they didn't bother him very much. Not with his parents close by to protect him.

All the same he was not terribly anxious to go to Mystery Island. Who knew what they might find there?

CHAPTER TWO

The next few weeks were busy ones for all the Bradys. Father Brady had to work late in his office on several architectural projects that had to be finished before the trip to Maine. The constant attention to details, the consultations with the men who had to build the shopping center he was designing, left him very tired at night.

Often by the time he arrived home he was even too tired to eat. Several times he had to remain in the office so late that he missed dinner entirely. He would phone ahead and tell Mother Brady to have their meal without him. Then, when he got home, he would speak briefly to the kids, hurriedly eat a sandwich and coffee in the kitchen, and retire to his study with a loaded briefcase.

At such times he was so intent on his work that some nights he fell asleep at his desk. He was certainly in no mood to revise the family's vacation plans.

When Mother Brady came in one night and asked him to do just that, he looked at her in astonishment.

"Carol, you must be joking. I'm up to my neck at the office. I haven't got time to look for places at the beach. And everything's been taken at the mountains. You know what it's like with the summer rush. You've got to grab things long in advance or they're gobbled up. I was talking to one of the men at the office about it this morning. He waited too long to book rooms for his family and now they have to wait an extra six weeks. He had to change all his vacation plans."

"I know, darling," she said. "It's just that I'm worried about the effect of all those pirate ghost stories on the children. Bobby and Cindy are especially affected. They found it hard to sleep most of last week."

"Why?" Mike Brady asked astonished. "It's just a story, for Pete's sake. Nobody really takes ghost stories seriously."

"At their age you do," Carol Brady said gently. "They have been taking it very seriously. And I must say that the other kids talking about it hasn't helped."

"What do they say?"

"Oh, Peter and Jan keep telling Bobby and Cindy that there are ghosts walking all over Mystery Island and that it's very dangerous to be out after dark. And they say the ghosts like to scare newcomers in particular because they don't want their privacy bothered. You know."

"Well, tell them to quit it," Mike Brady said.

15

"I don't want any more of it. And I'm too busy to plan anything else. We'll have a fine time there, all of us. There's a beautiful cottage, great swimming—everything. And no ghosts. Tell those mischief-makers to stop scaring Bobby and Cindy or I'll throw a scare into them!"

But it didn't stop Peter and Jan. The next night both children thought of a new way to frighten Bobby and Cindy. They took some clean bedsheets from the linen closet and put them over their heads. Slowly they crept up to where Bobby and Cindy were sleeping.

Peter began to moan. "Wha . . . wha . . . wha . . . Oooooh!" Jan began to make funny little noises that sounded very eerie.

"Eeeeeeeh . . . aaaaaaaaaaah . . . ohhhhhhhhhhhh!"

When Bobby and Cindy did not awaken at first, they made the sounds louder. Slowly Cindy's eyes opened and looked around her. In the dark, she could see nothing at first. Then to her amazement she made out a white shape without a head and it was walking slowly toward the bed!

At the same moment Bobby awoke and stared ahead of him with horror. There in the room, directly in front of him was a shape that could only be a ghost. It was pale white, it had no eyes or mouth or face, and it was moving and making weird, horrible noises!

Both children immediately jumped out of bed and with wild yells ran directly into their parents' bedroom.

16

"Mother, Mother, Daddy . . . There's ghosts here! Wake up! Wake up!" Cindy was almost beside herself with fear.

"They're coming after us," Bobby shouted, shaking his father. Mike Brady was so tired that he did not respond at first and Bobby had to shake his father much harder. When he finally peeled one eye open, he found his two youngest children jumping up and down with fright. He sat up in bed astonished, as did his wife.

"What on earth is going on?" he demanded.

"Ghosts! Ghosts!" Cindy shouted into his ear. "We just saw them. All white and making strange, awful noises."

"Just awful!" Bobby agreed. The two parents stared at their children. They were obviously very frightened and both talking at once, as if hearing the sound of their own voices made them feel better.

"Hey, calm down!" Mike Brady said firmly. "You're all right. You just had a bad dream."

"No," Cindy yelled. "We saw them. We both saw them. They were dressed in white and they were walking right at us. We just ran out in time. One more second and they would have caught us."

"Did you hear anything, Carol?" Father Brady asked.

"No!" She said.

"We did," another voice announced from the doorway. The Bradys looked around and saw Greg and Marcia with their arms around two figures clad in bedsheets.

"Here are your two ghosts," Marcia said smiling.

"Yeah, we found them prowling around the hall," Greg added.

Cindy and Bobby regarded the two white figures with caution. Were they dangerous even if they were captured, they wondered? Besides they had heard that ghosts could slip out of anything. They were free as air, weren't they, and just as solid? The youngest Bradys moved even closer to their parents and away from the scary looking figures.

"Let's get a better look at them," Mr. Brady said briskly.

He nodded to Marcia and Greg, who promptly took the sheets off the two figures, revealing two very embarrassed looking children.

"What's all this about, Peter and Jan?" Mr. Brady asked very sternly.

Peter blushed deeply and stared guiltily at his sister. "We were just playing a little joke, that's all," he offered.

"A little joke that terrified your brother and sister and woke us all up," his father reminded him.

"We didn't mean anything wrong or bad," Jan said quickly. "They shouldn't have got so scared. I didn't know they were such little babies as all that."

"Don't call us babies," Cindy said angrily.

"Yeah. Shut up!" added Bobby. "I think Daddy ought to punish you for waking up the whole house."

Mike Brady's eyebrows raised and he turned to the other children and his wife.

"What do you think the proper punishment ought to be for impersonating a ghost?" he asked. "Should we double the chores they have this week?"

"Maybe we ought to leave them behind when we go to Mystery Island," Greg said in a joking tone. "We can always send the two of them to camp instead."

The joking tone was lost on the two culprits.

"Oh please no, Daddy . . . don't do that," Jan pleaded.

"We promise not to do it again—ever," Peter added.

Mike Brady waited a moment and then turned to Cindy and Bobby.

"Shall we take these two secondhand ghosts to Mystery Island with us, Bobby and Cindy? I'll leave it up to you."

"Please," Peter asked, looking at Bobby and Cindy with eyes that begged forgiveness. "We were only kidding. We didn't mean to scare you so much."

"Okay, they can come," Bobby said finally.

"Yeah, it's okay," Cindy added. "But you'd better not try anything like that again."

The rest of the time till they left there were no more practical jokes and no kidding about spirits. Occasionally, Bobby and Cindy would open their eyes warily in the darkness and stare about them. But nothing white or any other color ever appeared and by common agreement the topic of ghosts was dropped from the family's conversations. Beside there was too much else to talk about.

What would they take along with them? Would summer clothing be enough or would it get cold in Maine? After all, islands in the Atlantic Ocean would be bound to be colder than the mainland. There were excited discussions about what sweaters and slacks were needed. Greg went shopping for some new jeans and Carol Brady took the girls for some new slacks and dresses that would hold up in the unpredictable Maine weather. She was careful to get waterproof raincoats for them as well.

Alice unpacked their rubbers and galoshes from a closet where they had lain unused for ages because she said they might come in handy.

"You can't tell how much rain there'll be there. I hear Maine's pretty wet sometimes in summer. A feller I met in the butcher's said it can sometimes rain several days on end, and if it does it can get mighty muddy, I can tell you that."

The last day was spent in packing and everyone pitched in. The children were responsible for their own toys. Even though they did not have to worry about the weight in their luggage, their parents cautioned them not to take too many of their playthings.

"There'll be lots to do on the island," Mr. Brady said. "And you don't want to get loaded down in advance. Also, it's too much trouble to move a lot of heavy luggage around. I'm not sure what kind of transportation is available on the island, and I don't think anyone wants to carry heavy bags a long distance."

So the Brady kids took only a couple of things apiece—things they just couldn't part with. Cindy took a small doll and a little ball she loved to play with. Bobby took some of his favorite cartoon books. Peter felt he just had to take along an adventure story he had been reading and Jan took along her watercolor set. Marcia contented herself with a small pocket radio and Greg with some of his favorite motor magazines.

The very last day the conversation at mealtime was so exciting the kids could barely eat their food. They were all so full of the impending trip that eating seemed too tame by comparison.

The Brady kids kept passing around some picture books about New England Mother Brady had brought home from a bookshop and Father Brady showed them some snapshots of the island taken by their host.

The pictures showed a beautiful island with a magnificent shoreline and many coves and indentations that looked like caves or secret places that pirates would love, places where boats might easily be kept out of sight or even disguised. There were some interesting looking rolling hills on Mystery Island, too, and all sorts of houses—brick houses, frame houses, and even some that looked as if they might be built from raw logs. These intrigued the children the most.

"I wonder who lives in those," Cindy asked, after examining pictures of such houses.

"Maybe pirates?" Peter joked. "They don't have time to lay bricks. Or maybe the original families of the pioneers live in them. They look like the kind of houses people put up when they don't have any tools."

"I don't think so," Marcia put in. "I've seen the houses the early visitors to New England built and they didn't look anything like that."

"Well, whatever it is," Bobby said, "it sure looks mysterious. That black color and all. Doesn't it, Greg?"

Greg smiled affectionately at his youngest brother and then nodded seriously. "Yes. It looks very mysterious. Like there might be men in there with loaded rifles ready for Indians to show up."

"You mean they got Indians on the island, too?" Cindy asked anxiously.

"No, of course not," Jan said firmly. "Can't you see Greg is just kidding you?"

Cindy did not look too sure, and the remark made the island seem more mysterious than ever. For a moment there was a silence as everybody thought of seeing Mystery Island for the first time the very next evening and wondered what they would discover. Then Mr. Brady broke into their thoughts crisply.

"Okay, everybody break out of their trance. We've got things to do. This is the last day for haircuts and the last day to buy anything we absolutely need. No more time for dawdling. Got to get moving."

The rest of the day seemed to move like an express train as the Bradys got haircuts and last minute things at the drug store and shops, made arrangements to stop the paper and have their mail picked up, and other things. They went to bed early because they had to catch the plane promptly at nine in the morning. But nobody slept much that night. There were just too many wonderful thoughts running around in their heads.

The next morning they were sorry they hadn't slept well because they had to get up at six and everyone felt very tired and grumpy. But the mood quickly disappeared as soon as the realization hit them that in three short hours they would be flying toward Maine and Mystery Island. Three short hours. Again the excitement of actually beginning a trip, of flying thousands of miles across the United States, of seeing the Atlantic Ocean buoyed them up enormously. They all felt as if they were starting out on a great adventure. And not just the kids—even the older Bradys and Alice were caught up in it.

Because of their excitement they couldn't stop talking, and once the car was underway they spoke more than ever—so much so that Father Brady had to ask them to be quiet so he could ask Mrs. Brady a question. But as soon as he finished, they started in again. Then suddenly, for no reason she could think of, just out of a wild impulse, Jan started to sing "Jingle Bells." She let the words come out loud and clear as if she was so full of them, she could not keep them down.

The other Brady kids stared at her in surprise for a minute. Then a moment later everybody in the car joined her in singing the Christmas song.

"That's what it really feels like," Cindy yelled with excitement. "Just like Christmas."

CHAPTER THREE

The flight across America seemed amazingly swift to them. How could anyone move that fast, Cindy wanted to know. The company jet wasn't as big as the ones they had seen on outings to the airport, but it was still huge. The pilot told them it easily accommodated thirty passengers and was used to take important businessmen and women to the different company offices across the continent.

Bobby listened to the man politely, but he was much more interested in getting a window seat and looking down at the clouds. With the blessing of their parents, the kids had been permitted to bring along small cameras, and as soon as they were in the plane they were busily snapping at everything that interested them: the stewardess, the pilot, the interior of the aircraft, and the clouds. There wasn't much else to take because the great billowing cloud masses curtained them from the ground below.

Not that it mattered. After an hour of flying

only Greg and Marcia were awake, and even they were nodding. By the time the plane landed in Maine, they had all taken airborne naps.

From the small airport to the ferry it was a bumpy ride over narrow roads surrounded by potato fields and interesting-looking brick and frame houses scattered here and there. The fields looked different than the ones they had seen in the big orange groves in California. They were hillier, for one thing, and dotted with rocks and boulders. The few men and women they saw at work at the end of the day looked very tired.

The ferry was a huge houseboat type vessel with the name MYSTERY ISLAND painted in big red letters on its side. It seemed impossibly dreary, with its dirty smokestack and rusting metal fixtures and the load of farmers and dusty cars it carried. But it did not look that way for long. Once the Bradys were well into the billowing waves of the Atlantic, the boat seemed to change for them into a kind of magic vehicle, an enchanted carpet transporting them to further adventures.

Bobby and Cindy kept running up and down the decks, shouting lustily at the waves, yelling things like "Look at that big one . . . wow . . . did you see that? It looks bigger than the ship." Peter and Jan took several snapshots of the dock and the speck of land in the distance that was obviously Mystery Island. Greg was more interested in the look of the vessel. After twenty minutes of studying the sea and the sky, he strolled over to the automobile area and talked to the driver of a fascinating-looking dune buggy.

"I didn't know they used those out here," he said conversationally. "They're very big in California. Lotta guys go out to the desert with them."

"They're big here, too," the owner, a tall, red-headed young man said smiling. "Especially where they have dunes, and we've got some great ones on Mystery. Maybe we don't have all your scenery here, but we got less smog."

Marcia found herself talking to a young girl about her own age who lived on the island and was coming back from school. She was a shy girl, and she had been reading quietly until Marcia spoke to her.

"About how long does the ferry take to get to Mystery Island?" Marcia asked, a little hesitantly. She was not sure whether she should interrupt the girl's reading as they sat on the long bench that faced the ship's windows.

"About an hour and half, I reckon," the girl said brusquely and turned back to her book. Marcia felt very foolish for having asked her the question and was about to move away and leave her undisturbed when the girl squinted at her and with the bare trace of a smile held out her hand.

"Name's Margy. Margy Blandon. What's yours?"

"Marcia Brady. . . . sorry I interrupted your reading."

"No problem. Brady, you said?"

"Yes."

The girl's eyes widened with new interest. "Then you must be the summer folks who are taking over the Arnold cottage."

"That's right," Marcia said smiling warmly. "How did you know?"

"Not much you don't know quick on Mystery. It's a small place and gossip moves fast. You ain't much on superstition then, I guess?"

"Why do you say that?" Marcia wanted to know.

"The Arnold place ain't been rented much since the doings three years back."

"What kind of doings?" Marcia asked apprehensively. The girl's steadfast gaze and her curt tone bothered her. Margy was looking at her as if she were a curiosity of some sort.

"Well, maybe you'll find out soon enough," Margy said mysteriously. "Ain't no use my scaring you now."

"No," Marcia said. "I'd really like to know. What happened at the cottage three years ago?"

Margy pursed her thin lips and squinched up her nose as if trying to make up her mind whether to tell her after all.

"You sure you want me to tell you?" she asked. "Folks are always saying it's bad trying to tell the summer people about the doings. It scares them off and hurts the shops and all. Gives the island a reputation we don't want."

"Please do tell me, Margy," Marcia pleaded. "I can't stand secrets when I only know half of them. And I promise not to be scared."

"Well, all right then. About three years ago

28

Mr. Arnold had some guests in from Chicago and they brought their dog and children and all. They nearly went out of their minds. Seeing all kinds of things at night and hearing things too."

"What kind of things?" Marcia insisted.

Margy Blandon wet her lips as she hesitated and then sighed. "Mrs. Roark, the mother, was strolling with the dog they brought along—near the water—when she heard singing behind her. She turned and saw a man dressed in pirate clothes coming right at her with a cutlass in his hand. She ran like the wind back toward the house. The next night Mr. Roark saw the same figure after the dog let out a big howl."

"What happened then?" Marcia asked. She was glad none of the younger Brady children were there.

"Mr. Roark seized a rifle from the house and fired several bullets at the figure. But he never got near him. Then for several nights after that they were wakened up by sea chanteys sung by men outside their windows and when they looked out, there was nobody out there. But the dog was howlin' terribly."

"There must be some explanation for all that," Marcia said lamely. "There are no such things as ghosts. Everybody knows that."

"Then what was all that stuff the Roarks saw? All their children nearly driven out of their heads—they couldn't sleep or nothing after that. Not that I blame them. Seeing pirates over two hundred years old, hearing them yell, seeing that dog howlin' at nothing they could make out in the dark."

"I still think there was an explanation," Marcia said. But she did not sound very convinced as she said the words.

"The only explanation folks on Mystery Island believe in," Margy Blandon snorted, "is that the summer people stirred up the spirits of the pirates who lived here. Everybody knows the pirates walk at night to guard their buried treasure and that they're suspicious of newcomers."

"Why didn't it happen before, then?" Marcia wanted to know.

"That's easy. Matt Arnold didn't rent out to summer people till three years ago. The cottage belonged to his grandparents and he came here as a boy. The ghosts consider him an islander because he had kin here and lived here for two years when he was a little boy."

"What about other summer people? Do they see or hear the same things?" Marcia asked. She looked around her to see if any of the other Brady children were nearby. On the other side of the deck she could make out Bobby and Cindy running madly and a little closer she spied Jan and Peter bent over the rail as they looked at the ocean. Her parents and Greg were nowhere to be seen.

"Did any of the other visitors report such sights or sounds?" she asked again.

"No," Margy said quietly, "but there's a good reason why the Roarks saw them, according to the oldtimers on the island."

"What is it?" Marcia asked.

30

"The Arnold cottage is almost exactly on the spot where Red Andrew had his house when he lived here. Of course the house burned to the ground a long time back—right after the American Revolution—but the island historical society has all the records. Matt Arnold's people built on the same site."

Marcia Brady felt chilled to the bone as she heard Margy's last words. They were going to live right on the same site!

"And that ain't all," Margy added, looking directly at her. "One reason the Roarks came to Mystery Island is because Mrs. Roark was distantly related to Red Andrew. She'd looked up the records and found out that Red Andrew lived here and had been searching for a place to rent for years.

"According to old man Harkness, your neighbor, the Roarks were brought here by the ghost of Black Tom. Drawn to the place like a magnet so he could do them harm."

"That's ridiculous," Marcia said in a quavering voice. "Even if that relationship was there, it was just a coincidence. It just happened to be that they were looking for a place here. I don't believe it possible for ghosts, even if they exist, to actually pull people to some place like that."

Margy smiled. "Maybe so, but then why pick the exact site where her kin lived? And why didn't anyone else see the ghosts or hear the sounds? I'll tell you why," Margy said, spearing at Marcia's dress with her bony forefinger. "Because the ghosts were out to scare her to death or drive her insane. If her husband hadn't got her out of here fast, it would have happened, too. As it was, she was in pretty bad shape, I can tell you."

"How?" Marcia asked.

"Why I saw that poor woman," Margy said indignantly. "And let me tell you, she was in a state of near collapse. Jumpy? That woman was as nervous as a cat. When my maw and I went in to see her shortly before they left, why she could barely talk. Her eyes were roaming the room, afraid to fix on anyone. She was still shaking. And they just lit out in a tearin' hurry. All except the dog—they left it behind with the woman who came to clean up."

"MYSTERY ISLAND!" a strong male voice boomed out behind them. "We'll be pulling into Black Tom's Cove in a few minutes."

The sound of Black Tom's name sent a chill down Marcia Brady's spine.

CHAPTER FOUR

"Oh, you were just being teased," Greg said when she repeated Margy's conversation. "Can't you tell when your leg's being pulled, Marcia?"

He looked at her with amusement as they sat together on the back of the station wagon that was waiting for them when they docked. Matt Arnold had thoughtfully arranged to have the island's garage owner put an almost new red station wagon at the Bradys' disposal.

"Hey, this is a great little wagon," Greg added, patting the leather interior. "I didn't expect a bus like this. I thought we'd get some battered up old jalopy or something."

He glanced at his sister's strained face. She was still thinking about the ghost legend.

"Aw, come on, Marcia," he said, tugging at her arm. "There's nothing to worry about. Forget it. There are no ghosts outside of movies."

"Lower your voice Greg!" she warned as she saw Bobby and Cindy turn curiously in their seats to look at them. "I don't want them all to hear or none of us will sleep tonight."

"Except me," Greg laughed. "I'll sleep like a baby. That ocean ride really wore me out."

He stopped as a big white cottage loomed up ahead of them. In the darkness, it looked immense.

"Everybody out," Mr. Brady yelled. "This is it."

The doors of the station wagon opened and nine tired but happy travelers emerged. They moved back several yards to examine the exterior of the place they would live in for the next few weeks.

"Terrific!" was Alice's first remark. "This place is a palace. Just look at it."

"It's wonderful and so big," Carol Brady exclaimed.

"I hope it isn't as cold inside as it is out here," Mr. Brady added, looking up at the two-story frame structure. The building was set on a hill that overlooked the ocean and was surrounded by broad green fields and hills as far as the eye could reach. A flight of stone steps descended from a cliff fifty yards from the house to a small white beach below.

"Hey, feel that ocean breeze," Peter said suddenly. "Boy, I'll bet it's fantastic flying a kite out here."

"Yes, if you don't get pulled over that cliff," his sister Jan said dryly. "And the way you run with a kite, I expect to find you down there the first time out."

"What's wrong with the way I run?" Peter

said, irritated by Jan's criticism. "I'm one of the fastest runners at school, and you know it."

"Okay, okay, I was just kidding, Peter," Jan said amiably. "Let's put some lights on. This place looks creepy in the dark."

Almost as if the house had heard her and was responding, several lights went on in the lower windows. The effect was so unexpected that it startled everybody.

"What was that?" Marcia asked worriedly. "I thought nobody lived here."

"That's what I thought," Mr. Brady said. "The garage man didn't say anything about anyone else being here when I took the key from him."

"Maybe there are ghosts," Greg said grinning broadly.

"Shut up, Greg, I don't think that's funny at all."

Cindy, Bobby, Peter, and Jan regarded Greg with widened eyes. Mrs. Brady gave him a frown and put her arms around the frightened children.

"Let's go find out who's in there," Mr. Brady said worriedly. "I hope Matt Arnold didn't get his wires crossed and invite two sets of visitors at once."

"If he did, we may have to sleep in the car," Peter said.

Just as Mr. Brady began to knock on the door it opened and a tall, robust-looking woman in her fifties opened it.

"Welcome to Arnold House, Mr. Brady," she said looking at him. The words were polite but no smile accompanied them. "I'm Mrs. Sullivan. I take care of the house winters when Mr.

Arnold's away. I thought you might want an evening meal so I prepared one."

"Why that's very nice," Mrs. Brady cried and then smiled at Alice. "I'm sure you're delighted, too. You thought you'd have to cook tonight, Alice. Hmm, that smells delicious."

She looked toward the kitchen from which steamy odors were coming. "Lobster stew, ma'am," Mrs. Sullivan said. "We catch a lot of lobsters here. And some mashed potatoes and deep-dish apple pie. I hope you'll find that pleasing."

"Pleasing?" Mr. Brady said, smiling at all of the by-now very hungry Brady children. "It's a delightful surprise. What about that, kids—a real Maine lobster dinner cooked by an expert. You thought you were all settling for hamburgers cooked by Alice, didn't you?"

He caught sight of Alice's annoyed expression and tapped her arm fondly. "Take it easy, Alice. All I meant is that no one in his right mind expected you to cook us a real dinner after traveling across the country and the ferry ride, too. You know how much we all love your cooking. Right, kids?"

The Brady kids chimed in with smiles and nods. Alice relaxed.

"Well, let's bring in the bags and take them upstairs. Then we can unpack after dinner."

The boys and Mr. Brady went out to the car while the women and girls inspected the premises. The cottage was astonishingly large inside, with spacious rooms and closets and long corridors. Although the tone was of the nineteenth century, the conveniences were all modern indeed. The bathrooms looked just like their own back home. As they wandered back down the stairs, the Brady girls heard a dog bark loudly down below.

"What's that?" Cindy asked with astonishment. "That sounds like a dog."

"That *is* a dog," Mrs. Sullivan said calmly.

The girls rushed downstairs and saw a beautiful big white dog in the doorway leading to the kitchen. The animal stared at them complacently. Marcia and Jan and Cindy exchanged smiles of delighted surprise. The dog was beautiful.

"What's his name, Mrs. Sullivan?" Jan cried.

"I don't really know," that lady said. "I just call him 'Dog.' He was left here by the Roarks."

"Oh, can he stay here with us?" little Cindy asked quickly. "I promise to take good care of him. We all will."

"Now wait a minute girls," Mrs. Brady said. "You can't expect Mrs. Sullivan to simply turn over her dog to you like that."

"That's quite all right," the housekeeper said in a flat, emotionless voice. "This is actually the only home the dog has ever had. He was left by those people and I felt it my duty to feed him. I couldn't just let him die of hunger. But my husband isn't very partial to animals around the house so I have to keep him in the garage. He'll be happier here with you, I'm sure."

"Oh, wonderful," the Brady girls said. "But we have to give him a name. What will we call him?"

"How about Friday?" Greg said from the

street door. He was looking at the dog with great interest as he held a suitcase in each hand.

"Why Friday? Jan asked.

"Yeah, that's a funny name to give a dog," Peter said.

"I know why," Bobby cried. "Because it's Friday."

"Right," Greg replied. "I think it's a groovy name. Don't you, Dad?"

"Why not?" he said. "It's easy to remember."

"If that is all, I'll leave now," Mrs. Sullivan said in her formal tone. "Best I get back to my husband now. He suffers from asthma."

"All right, thank you very much for the welcoming meal," Mrs. Brady said warmly. "I'm sure we're all grateful to you."

"Especially me," popped up Alice, her eyes twinkling. "I'm about ready to drop in my tracks."

"If you need me for anything, I live near the village," Mrs. Sullivan said. "Anyone can tell you where it is. Or you can telephone. You can find a good shopping center for food and all at the village."

"Do we have any neighbors we should say hello to? That you can introduce us to?" Mrs. Brady inquired.

"Are there any kids here?" Peter asked quickly.

"Well . . ." Mrs. Sullivan hesitated. "There is a man who lives fairly close to you and there are two teen-aged children. Jonathan Harker is the man's name. But I'm not sure he'll be partial to visitors. He's an elderly gentleman, very sharp-tongued, and keeps to himself mostly. His house

38

is on a big hill just out of sight of this house. His grounds are fenced in."

"What about the children?" asked Marcia. "Don't they ever get out?"

"Sometimes," Mrs. Sullivan said. "They belong to his housekeeper, Mrs. Adams. I must leave now. I'll be back each Friday to help with the cleaning, as Mr. Arnold requested."

Without another word, she turned on her heel and moved toward the door.

"Just a minute," Mrs. Brady said. "Why did Mr. and Mrs. Roark abandon such a lovely animal?"

For a moment the housekeeper did not reply. Her eyes were plainly troubled by the question.

"Yeah, why?" Peter asked curiously.

"Because Mrs. Roark felt that the dog was possessed by evil spirits," Mrs. Sullivan answered finally.

"Possessed by evil spirits?" Mr. Brady repeated.

"Let's go back to California," Alice said. "The only thing evil there is the smog."

"Wait a minute. I want to hear about this," Mr. Brady said.

Mrs. Sullivan told them essentially the same tale that Marcia had heard from Margy Blandon on the ferry.

"Mrs. Roark was troubled by the fact that the dog continued to bark into the darkness all night after she saw the spirits," Mrs. Sullivan explained. "She was convinced that the ghosts had entered into the animal itself. That they were forcing the dog to bark that way."

"Well, didn't anyone try to straighten her out?" Greg asked.

"No, sir," Mrs. Sullivan said. "She was doing very poorly at the time and Mr. Roark feared he would drive her over the edge if he persisted in trying to convince her she was wrong. You must remember the poor woman was frightened out of her wits by what she saw."

"Or thought she saw," Mrs. Brady said.

"And I'm sure there are a lot of superstitious folk on the island," Mr. Brady added.

"Yes, sir, there are." Mrs. Sullivan's blue eyes flashed ominously. "But maybe there's good reason for them to be."

"What do you mean, Mrs. Sullivan?" Marcia asked uneasily.

"Nothing maybe," Mrs. Sullivan said tartly, "except that mainlanders don't know the answers to everything and people on Mystery Island are not all fools."

"Meaning, I guess, that you do believe in the pirate ghosts," Mr. Brady said, eyeing the housekeeper's face.

"Aye, I do." In another second she was out the door and had closed it firmly behind her.

"Wow," Peter said, looking through the window as Mrs. Sullivan strode away from the house. "She scares me almost as much as the ghosts."

"She isn't exactly the soul of good cheer," Mr. Brady said. "Come on, let's see if she can cook. That's more important. And if you don't come in with me now, I'm going to eat that whole lobster thing by myself. I'm starved to death."

The lobster stew was the most delicious sea-food dish they had ever eaten and Alice was promptly requested to ask Mrs. Sullivan for the recipe.

"Don't count on her giving it to me," Alice said, pulling a long face. "She doesn't volunteer things easily."

"Tell her you'll sic old Black Tom on her if she doesn't give it to you," Greg laughed.

A moment after he said it he was sorry. Both Cindy and Bobby looked anxiously at him.

"Oh, come on, you babies," he teased. "There's nothing to be afraid of."

"Don't call us babies," Bobby cried annoyedly. "I'm eleven years old."

"And I'm ten," Cindy chimed in. But Greg's words had obviously found a target. Mrs. Sullivan's remarks were troubling the two youngest Brady children.

They remained troubled during the rest of what seemed to them to be the longest night of their lives. As they lay in their beds later, both children stared at the ceiling for over an hour. Every sound was amplified until it seemed to be coming from some giant being. The noise of the crickets outside their windows seemed terribly loud to them, so loud they could not close their eyes.

Although Marcia, Greg, Jan, and Peter pretended they were not at all concerned over the ghost legend, it affected them, too. What if it were true, they wondered as they lay in the darkness. What if the ghosts of Black Tom and Red Andrew and their pirate crews were still reenacting the battle they had fought hundreds of years earlier? They kept expecting to see the faces of the pirates loom in front of them and the more they expected it, the realer the thing became.

As she finally slept, Jan began to dream of the pirates. In her dream Black Tom appeared in the room as large as life, a huge bearded man with black hair and beetling, thick black eyebrows and dark eyes like ebony buttons. In his hand he held a cutlass and he limped around the room on a wooden peg-leg.

As the figure moved closer to her bed, Jan woke up and screamed out loud. Instantly the other children woke up and crowded over to her side. In another moment the elder Bradys and Alice were in the room as well.

"What happened, darling?" Mrs. Brady asked anxiously. "Are you all right?"

"I saw Black Tom's ghost," Jan cried. "He was standing right over my bed."

Mr. Brady shook his head as he rubbed his daughter's hand. "You saw nothing of the kind, Jan. You were having a dream."

"No," Jan protested. "I could smell his breath. He was standing right over me. I mean it."

"You were having a nightmare," her father insisted. "Now go back to sleep, everyone, and I don't want any more talk about ghosts. Is that clear?"

In a few moments all the Brady children were asleep again or, rather, trying to be. It wasn't easy. All of them were wondering the same thing. Had Jan had a dream after all? Or was it actually

Black Tom in person? Even if it had been a dream, could Black Tom had forced her to dream of him? Had he made himself appear in Jan's dream?

Jan was not sure herself. The nightmare had been so vivid to her. And now every sound, every flicker of light seemed magnified a thousand times. As the night progressed, they all heard doors squeak and the wooden floors creak in a way that thoroughly alarmed them. At intervals they would hear the wind whistle outside. After the first few times, Peter and Jan both sat up in their beds listening.

Peter was certain now that the house was haunted. Jan wanted to run out of the room but she was afraid of her parents' reaction if she did. In another moment the constant groanings and creakings of doors and floor boards had made all six Brady children sit up worriedly and wait to see what would happen next. To see if the pirate ghosts would appear.

For a long time they listened as silently as possible. Cindy and Bobby would have held their breaths if they could have, because they feared the pirates would hear them. The silence was eerie in a way because all of the kids expected something to break it. Bobby and Cindy expected to see great armies of bearded pirates like those they had seen in book illustrations and television cartoons come bursting into the room, knives at the ready. Jan thought there would be just Black Tom, and Peter expected Black Tom and Red Andrew to fight it out again.

As for Marcia and Greg, they did not know

exactly what they would find, but they expected something. Mrs. Sullivan's words had filled them with dread, too. For what seemed an endless time nothing happened, and then they saw the strange lights. And after the lights came the weird, scary sounds.

The lights appeared at first as flickering movements on the ceiling. Then they transferred to the windows of their rooms. At first the children lay shivering in their beds, wondering whether the lights signified the arrival of the ghosts.

As he trembled in his bed, Peter fought the urge to bolt out of his room and rush to his parents. Then as he looked up from under the tip of his coverlet, which was nearly over his whole face, he thought he saw something flash across the window pane. The sight of it made him so nervous, he dove under the coverlet and held his breath.

After a minute or two he had to come up for air and as he did he peeked carefully at the window again. What he saw chilled him to the marrow. In the window was a huge, bearded face with cunning black eyes and a sneering expression. The eyes were the biggest Peter had ever seen. In the man's ear was a golden earring such as he had frequently seen in pictures of pirates.

At almost the same time, Peter heard a strange moan that seemed to come from the walls themselves or from the window. The sound was the weirdest he had ever heard in his whole life, as if someone were crying out for help. Or else as if the maker of the sound were in some terrible pain.

That was all Peter needed. He jumped up out of bed and ran toward the door in a pell-mell, headlong rush to get out of there.

"Wait," he heard Greg yell hoarsely. "Where you going?"

"To get Dad," Peter said breathlessly. "I just saw a pirate's face in the window."

Greg shook his head. "There's nothing at the window."

Peter looked. "Not now, maybe, but before I saw it."

"Are you positive you saw it?" Greg asked carefully.

Peter stared at the window again and then at his older brother. He was not sure any longer. Could he have simply imagined the entire thing as Bobby had a little earlier?

"I don't invent things like that," Peter said hesitantly.

"I didn't say you do," Greg said. "But, Pete, we're all in a tizzy here tonight. We're tired from the trip and Mrs. Sullivan got us all mixed up with that ghost stuff. You could have imagined it. Right?"

"I don't know," Peter admitted. Suddenly he heard the weird sound again—the same one he had heard before—the crying, painful-sounding moan.

"What about those sounds?" Peter looked at Greg. "Do you hear that, or am I out of my head?"

"No, I hear it," Greg said uneasily. "But maybe it's——." Before he could finish the sentence, Marcia, Bobby, Jan, and Cindy all ran into the room in their pajamas.

"There's a crazy sound!" Cindy kept saying. "Did you hear it?"

"I heard it," Jan said. She looked very serious.

Greg looked at his younger sister. "Jan, did you? I mean, this sound isn't one of your little practical jokes now, is it?"

"Me?" Jan asked astonished.

"I mean you didn't bring along some whistle or something to give out such sounds?" Greg persisted. "Because if you did . . ."

"I didn't do anything," Jan protested. "And I don't like being pointed out like this. I just heard the same noise you did, that's why I'm here."

"Well, you do things like this back home. Remember when you imitated an owl and scared poor Cindy half to death?" Marcia said gently.

"Or the time you kept barking like a dog," Bobby recalled, "and we all thought a dog had snuck into the house?"

Jan's face grew red as she listened. "I know. I did that. As a joke. But I didn't do these sounds. I mean it."

She looked pleadingly at her brothers and sisters. Greg nodded finally. "Okay. You didn't do it. But someone did. And maybe somebody pressed his face against the window while Pete was looking. We gotta do something."

"Let's get Daddy," Cindy cried excitedly.

"No," Greg said. "We can't wake them up again. Not after Bobby's thing. They'd just get

46

very grumpy and we'd have a terrible morning tomorrow. I've got an idea. Let's all go downstairs together and look around."

"You mean all by ourselves?" Bobby asked worriedly.

"That sounds very dangerous," Peter said.

"Not if we're all together," Greg insisted. "There'll be six of us."

He looked around him. "Well, who's willing to go with me?"

There was a moment of silence when no one answered. Then Marcia put her arm on Greg's and said quietly, "I'm with you." The other Brady kids looked at each other uneasily. Each of them was feeling guilty inside at the thought they were letting Greg and Marcia do it alone.

The idea of ghost hunting on Mystery Island after midnight did not sit very well with any of them. But the idea of leaving it to the oldest children was too much. They had to back them up no matter how scared they felt. Peter spoke his feelings first.

"Look, I think we ought to all do this together. After all, we are a family and we ought to act together."

All of them were remembering that not long ago they were two separate families. The girls had had no father and the boys had had no mother. They had felt lonely, somehow, unfulfilled. The boys had often wondered what it would be like to have sisters of their own. The three girls had often pondered what fun they could have with brothers around to play with.

Now they were all together in one big happy

group and they all felt that they had to stick together in a crisis like this.

"I agree with Peter," Jan said very seriously. "I'm with Greg and Marcia, too."

In another second or two the others chimed in. Greg's face broke out into a grateful smile and he motioned to the others to follow him quietly. They descended the stairway slowly, seeing and hearing nothing but feeling very frightened every step of the way.

When they reached the living room downstairs they saw a strange-looking shape in one corner and for an instant the old terror came back. The shape looked very menacing in the dark.

"Look!" Cindy whispered.

Greg approached it cautiously and took a close look.

"It's Friday, the dog," he said, obvious relief in his voice. "He's sleeping, I think."

The sound of the children's voices woke him up very quickly, however, and he shook himself and came up on his feet. He looked at them quietly, showing neither interest nor indifference. The atmosphere of fear obviously had not reached him at all. He did not seem to think anything was wrong in the household.

All of a sudden, as the younger children patted the dog's mane, the weird sounds they had heard upstairs returned in full force. The long moaning sounds reverberated throughout the downstairs area chilling them all.

"What is that awful sound?" Cindy asked frightenedly.

"I'm scared," Bobby added quickly, getting closer to his older brothers and sisters. Greg put his arm around him to comfort him. Marcia held Cindy closer and stroked her hair gently.

"I don't know what that sound is," Greg said. "Let's go outside and see if we can find out."

"Oh, do we have to?" Cindy asked. "It's very dark out there. We don't know who might be out there waiting."

"There's no other way," Greg insisted. "Can't you see that's where it's coming from? We've got to go out to find out where it's coming from."

He looked at them all for a moment, then without another word opened the front door and stepped outside. As he did, they could all hear the booming surf of the sea against the rocks not far from the house.

Without a word they followed him. They had no idea who or what would face them outside, But they would soon find out.

CHAPTER FIVE

Outside it was as black as pitch for a moment and they all shivered as the cool ocean breeze knifed at their pajama-covered bodies. Even the dog seemed to tremble.

"Wow!" Cindy said. "I've never seen it so dark."

"That's cause you've never been up this late, dum dum," Peter told her. But he was made uneasy by the blackness of the night, too.

Then suddenly they all heard the loud moaning sounds again and they huddled together for protection. Fortunately the stars came out just then as some heavy cloud banks passed over them. It became lighter and their spirits lifted, too. Now it did not seem so bad after all. It was not too cold outside, and the whole thing had a kind of sense of adventure about it.

Greg motioned for them to follow him over the next hill and they did. As they reached the crest, they could see another hill not too far away. On it was a big house surrounded by a fence and perched almost at the edge of the cliff overlooking the ocean.

"This must be the Harker house," Marcia said. All of them examined the huge weather-beaten old mansion which seemed to hug the rocky soil like some enormous animal. The building, with its many wings and dark-wooded exterior, seemed to go on endlessly. There was a mysterious, brooding quality about its ugly gables and weathervane.

As they stared at the house, the light suddenly went on in one of the top story windows and they saw a man's figure frozen in the yellow light. They all drew back involuntarily because the sight was so unexpected. They saw the figure raise the window and then, holding a pair of binoculars, scour the area where they were standing.

"He's looking straight at us," Jan whispered. "Who is that?"

"Probably old man Harker," Peter said.

"Let's hide," Cindy suggested in a frightened voice as the series of moaning sounds resumed again.

"What on earth for?" Marcia said impatiently. "We're not doing anything wrong. It's a free country. If we want to walk along the cliff at night it's our business, so long as we aren't trespassing on his land."

As they watched the lighted window, the light was extinguished. Without anyone giving instructions, all of the Brady children continued to walk in the direction of the great dark house. It was as if they were lured by some giant magnet.

The house looked hideous in its black isolation with those incessant moaning sounds as it natural music. But the children were somehow smitten with a longing to see it up close. It was as if the house had a personality of its own and held all who came near it in a kind of spell.

They walked quietly for a few moments until they were within a few yards of the big fence around the house. Then, as if by common consent, they stopped.

"I'm scared," Cindy said, her lisp becoming more pronounced.

Before they could do or say anything more, the gate in the fence opened about fifty yards from where they stood. A figure somewhat camouflaged by a poncho or some sort of cloak around his shoulders stood there and regarded them silently.

"Who is that?" Peter asked.

"I don't know and I'm not going to find out," Jan said firmly.

"I'll find out," Greg said. He moved a little closer to the gate to get a better look at the sentinel-like figure.

"Let me look, too," Bobby said suddenly. He could not see the figure too clearly over Greg's shoulder.

As they regarded the newcomer, they saw him raise a long object in their general direction.

"What's he got there?" Bobby asked worriedly.

"It's a gun," Greg said quickly. "Move back! Wait a minute, I'd better talk to him."

But before he could say a word, the gun went off.

"Get down on the ground, everybody," Greg commanded. "Lie absolutely flat on your stomach so he can't see you."

When he saw Cindy still standing and looking at him uncertainly, he grabbed his sister's shoulders and pushed her gently but firmly to the ground.

"Stay put now, Baby," he ordered. "And don't be scared." He looked around him. Five figures lay prone on the dark ground. He stood up slightly and yelled out.

"Hey, what's going on? We're not doing anything. What are you firing at us for?"

In reply he was greeted with another bullet. Again the bullet came nowhere near them. It had apparently been fired up in the air. Had it been merely a warning shot, he wondered?

"Will you cut that out mister," Greg yelled out. "We've got children here. What's the matter with you? We live at the Arnold house. We're his tenants for the summer."

There was complete silence from the rifleman. Greg pondered the situation carefully. If the man were intent on shooting them, he had better get his brothers and sisters away from there fast. He decided that the best plan was to have them all crawl along the ground so that the man could not aim his gun properly in the darkness.

"Listen carefully now, all of you," Greg told them, kneeling close to their flattened bodies. "I don't know who this guy is, but he may be dangerous. I want you all to point your faces back to our house and crawl quickly back in that direction. Don't stand up no matter what you do,

53

unless I give the order. If I do I want you to stand up and then run like the wind toward our place.

"Everybody got that clear now?" Greg demanded.

When he got the answers he had requested, he commanded them all to start crawling. As they moved along the ground they all trembled. What if the man started firing at them? They moved in the expectation of hearing more bullets fly at them. But nothing happened. After a few minutes of snaking their way up and down the hilly terrain, they were nearly exhausted. To make it worse, the wind sprang up behind them and a cold spray from the ocean struck their thinly clad backs.

"Okay, get up and run for the house," Greg said suddenly. "We're out of sight of him now."

As they stood up and sprinted toward their own house like so many deer, they heard a male voice booming behind them.

"Next time stay off my land," the voice yelled angrily. "Don't come stalking around my place at night unless you want to get hurt!"

CHAPTER SIX

The next morning Mr. and Mrs. Brady learned the secret of the strange sounds they had all heard the night before. The man who told them was the storekeeper in town, a friendly old man with a thick thatch of gray hair who operated an all-purpose market and was a treasure house of knowledge about Mystery Island.

"Glad to meet you, folks," he said affably as they introduced themselves. "I got a letter from Mr. Arnold asking me to extend you credit privileges. Be glad to. Anything you like."

"Oh, no, no," Mike Brady said. "We'll pay for anything we buy. Mr. Arnold's been good enough as it is."

"Nope," Mr. Brownall said. "Be glad to. You're Mr. Arnold's friends. That's enough for me. Can't take your money. Now tell me how I can help you."

"I am paying you," Mike Brady said stubbornly. "But you can help us with a little information."

"Whatever you want to know," the old man said agreeably. "I've been here all my life. Know the history, people, everything. What I don't know I can find out from some old-timers here."

"Where are all those ghastly moaning sounds coming from," Carol Brady asked. "They scared our children half to death. And us as well."

"And Alice," Mr. Brady reminded her. "She locked herself in the bathroom with a steam iron in her hand most of the night."

Mr. Brownall laughed till his stomach heaved. "Those strange sounds come from a network of caves underground. You see, Mystery Island is honeycombed with them. The caves hold the wind and then let it out with that characteristic noise."

The grocer laughed. "Sometimes newcomers to the place go clear out of their minds the first few nights. Especially after hearing all about the pirate legends. We have a lot of practical jokers who make it worse by sometimes putting in special whistles in those caves.

"I remember about thirty-five years ago, there was a party of millionaires came up in a big yacht and lorded it over the whole population. Treated us all like dirt . . . you know, common servants who had to do their bidding. Old Charley Wellsley put a big steamboat whistle in one of the caves and blew the heck out of it between the cave's natural wind sounds. Right under the Brent Estate where they were staying.

"Well, sir, about three A.M. old Charley and his friends dressed in pirate costumes and wielding cutlasses came screaming down the road.

56

They had torches and all and those mainlanders nearly went berserk. They lit out of those windows and doors like howlin' banshees and ran so fast for their boat, they left their shoes behind. And lots more."

The grocer paused, laughing loudly at the memory of their headlong rush toward the sea.

"Old Charley and his friends don't still play these jokes, do they?" Mike Brady asked curiously.

"Nope. Charley's long since passed away. Why? You been troubled that way?"

Mr. Brady told him about the face in the children's window. Mr. Brownall looked serious for a moment.

"Don't have a clue who that might be. But I can ask around. Could be anybody. Or else——"

"Or else the real pirate ghosts," Mr. Brady said. "Is that what you meant?"

Mr. Brownall nodded solemnly.

At that instant, the Brady children filed into the store. Bobby and Cindy immediately repaired to the candy counter. Marcia and Jan checked the suntan lotions and sunglasses. Greg looked at some motor magazines on a rack while Peter browsed through a comic book. Carol Brady came to a decision when she saw them come into the store.

"Mr. Brownall," she began. "Someone fired a gun near my children last night as they walked by the shore. Near a big old house surrounded by a tall fence. Have you any idea who that might be?"

57

"Yep," Brownall said. "Why do you want to know?"

"Because I may complain to the police," she said.

"Was it close to the Arnold property or near the fence?" the grocer inquired. "That's important."

"Well, they were close to the fence," Mr. Brady said, "but I don't see what difference that makes."

"Lots of difference," Brownall said. "Old man Harker owns land stretching way past that fence and he's got a right to warn off poachers. He's a mighty nervous man at night. Usually he just fires a couple of warning blasts in the air. But sometimes he gets very angry and shoots straight at a target.

"Wounded a young man last summer who was on his land. Hit him in the arm. Since then his housekeeper—that's Maude Adams—has been able to keep a rein on the old man's temper. She and her two kids, Sybil and John, are the only real family poor man's got since his wife died years ago."

Brownall wet his lips and looked steadily at the Bradys. "Take my advice, Mr. and Mrs. Brady. Better leave old Harker alone. He's a very unsociable type. Very grouchy and he doesn't cotton to——"

The grocer broke off embarrassedly as the street door swung open and admitted an older woman and two teen-agers. The newcomers nodded coldly to the shopkeeper and busied themselves with some items on the crowded shelves.

58

"That's them," Brownall whispered. "Mrs. Adams and Sybil and John. I sure hope they didn't hear me talk about old man Harker. Excuse me a moment."

Brownall busied himself in the back of the shop as all the Bradys examined the visitors with undisguised interest. Greg was especially impressed with the girl, a slim, pretty creature who was the most beautiful young person he had seen in a long time. He sensed that she was aware of him, too, by the way her eyes managed to brush his every so often.

"Oh come on, Greg," Marcia whispered teasingly. "Stop looking at her like that or people will think you've got a crush on her."

"What are you talking about, silly," Greg said grumpily. "You don't know what you're saying." But his heart was beating much faster and he had a great desire to talk to her. For a long moment he hesitated. Then he made up his mind and holding a motor magazine in his hand, he went up to the girl.

"Excuse me, miss. My name's Greg. Greg Brady. Just moved into Matt Arnold's house for the summer. Can you tell me whether they have any auto races or boat races on Mystery Island this month?"

"Oh, brother," Marcia said, wincing as she heard Greg. "That sounds so terribly corny," she whispered to Peter.

The girl Greg addressed smiled at him.

"Well, I think they have boat races in about a week on the other side of the island."

"Really?" Greg said excitedly. "That's great!

Maybe you can show me where they're held. My dad's got a car and maybe we can drive over there."

The girl's smile was cut short by Mrs. Adams' announcement that they had to leave. The boy with them looked coolly at the Bradys and left. Sybil seemed to be embarrassed by her mother's action.

"My name's Sybil," she said. "I'm glad to meet you."

She left quickly.

CHAPTER SEVEN

Mike Brady patted Greg's arm sympathetically as they finished lunch, a lovely seafood dish made by Alice.

"Don't take it so hard son," said Mr. Brady. "It's a small island. I'm sure you'll see Sybil again."

"Where?" Greg said in a depressed voice. "I certainly can't just drop in on her. Harker would probably chase me out with a gun for trespassing."

"Well, he can't shoot you for walking on the beach," Alice said brightly. "And I'll bet if you look for her, she'll be there. Swimming or something."

Greg brightened immediately. "Hey, that's right." But a second later he looked sad again. "There must be a million beaches, though. How do I know which one she goes to?"

"Try Cambridge Beach," Alice said. "A woman over in the butcher shop told me all the teen-aged kids go there. They play guitars and surf and all. It's about a half mile from here."

Greg moved so fast they hardly saw him leave the house. He looked so excited that the elder Bradys, Alice, Marcia, and Jan burst out laughing. Cindy and Bobby wondered what they were all giggling about. Since they were anxious to get outdoors themselves, they asked permission to look at the sea.

"Good idea," Mr. Brady said. "Hey, why don't you guys take Friday with you? He needs a little exercise, anyway, and maybe he can act as a guide. He probably knows this area pretty well."

A moment later, with the dog in tow, Bobby and Cindy set out to explore the area near the Arnold house.

"Don't be too long now, children," Mrs. Brady called out after them as they left. "I thought we'd all take a drive in about an hour or so."

Their father had been right. Friday did know the area pretty well. At first they tried to guide him but when they saw that the dog had his own choices, they gave up and followed his lead.

"He sure seems to know where he wants to go," Cindy said. "Wonder where he's taking us?"

For a long time, Friday seemed to be taking them nowhere. If anything, the dog seemed to be moving in large circles. He would move over several sand dunes near the sea and then push back further inland. Finally, however, the dog led them back to the shoreline. They began to follow the edge of the water just below the Harker mansion.

"Maybe we'd better go back," Cindy said when

she noticed the house. Mr. Harker might come after us."

"I don't think he will," Bobby said bravely. "He just goes after people at night. Anyway, I'm not afraid of him."

To prove it, Bobby began to move ahead, looking back regularly at the Harker house to see if anyone was watching him. His I-dare-you attitude made his sister laugh at him. Suddenly she noticed something.

"Hey, Bobby. Look Friday's stopped."

They stared at the dog with interest. The animal had stopped in his tracks and was pawing eagerly at a large clump of bushes just at the foot of the cliff.

"What's he doing that for?" Bobby asked curiously.

"I don't know," Cindy replied. "Maybe it's his secret hiding place. Where he puts his bones or something he wants to keep." Suddenly a chipmunk ran past into the bushes.

"Let's get closer and see what it is," Bobby said.

As they bent over the dog, they failed to see their brother Greg as he passed them. Greg had given up on Sybil for the day. She was not at Cambridge Beach and none of the kids had seen her there recently. Somewhat sadly he walked along the shoreline, stopping occasionally to throw stones into the sea. He was disappointed but after a few good throws, he felt better. What the heck, he thought, she's not the only good-looking girl in the world.

When he got back to California, there'd be

plenty of girls at school. Anyway, he'd only be here for the summer so nothing with Sybil could last very long.

At the foot of the cliff, Cindy and Bobby watched as Friday suddenly slid through the bushes and vanished. Bobby parted the bushes. They hid the mouth of a cave!

"We'll have to go after him," Bobby told Cindy. "He went into a cave."

"I'm not going in there," she said.

"Come on," he said. "We can't just leave Friday there."

He led the way into the dark interior and after a moment Cindy followed. For a few minutes they moved through the darkness, calling out Friday's name. Finally when they were some distance from the cave opening and unable to see daylight, Cindy begged Bobby to lead them both out to the beach again.

"I can't," Bobby confessed after a long pause. "I can't find the entrance. You know what? I think we're lost."

Barry Williams and Chris Knight

Barry, Susan Olsen and Eve Plumb

Eve, Maureen, Barry and Susan

Barry

Maureen

Eve

Chris and Mike

CHAPTER EIGHT

A little after Cindy and Bobby had entered the mouth of the cave, Peter began to explore the area near the Arnold house. For a while he wandered about alone. Then he heard his sister Jan hailing him from a distance.

"Hey, where are you going?" she asked.

"I don't know. Just looking around," Peter said. "I was thinking of maybe trying to start up a seashell collection. I bet they got some fantastic shells in this place."

"Oh, that's a great idea," Jan cried. "Wait, I'll go with you. Let me get my swimsuit on first."

"Okay, but hurry."

For the next half hour Peter and Jan skirted the shoreline, stooping at odd intervals to pick up interesting-looking shells. They found pink ones and blue ones and yellow ones. They came in all shapes and sizes. Some of them were so tiny they fit neatly into the palm. Others were enormous.

"Hey, look at this one," Jan yelled, picking up

a shell that looked like a big cereal bowl. "This would be great for Dad's office. He could keep paper clips and rubber bands in it."

"Yeah," Peter said admiring it. "That's beautiful. I wonder if there are any more like——"

He stopped as he saw a figure approaching them. Some sixth sense told him to duck behind a rock and to pull Jan down beside him.

"Keep still," he ordered.

"Why?" she asked.

"I think I've seen this man's face somewhere."

"Where?"

"I'm not sure," Peter said. Then as the man came close, he knew. It was the face he had noticed at his window the night before.

"It's him, the guy I saw at the window last night," Peter said excitedly. "What's he doing here? He's coming from someplace near our house."

They remained there for a moment, holding their breaths. Then Jan's curiosity got the better of her and she raised her head to look at the man. Her brother tried to pull her down quickly but it was too late—the newcomer had seen her head bob up. Suddenly, he turned on his heel and made a dash for a group of boats anchored in a cove nearby.

"Why didn't you stay down?" Peter said annoyed. He jumped up and followed the man, but the intruder had already got a big headstart. By the time Peter and Jan reached the cove, he was jumping into a motorboat. A second later, he started the motor.

They stood on shore as the boat receded into the horizon, getting smaller and smaller.

"Who was it?" Jan asked.

"I don't know," Peter said. "But I don't like it. And he was definitely coming from someplace near our house. I'm going back to tell Dad, okay?" Jan nodded and said she was going to walk down the beach for a while.

When Peter got to their house, he saw a white envelope stuck beneath the street door. Someone had started to push it in and then changed his mind. Peter stooped to pick it up. It was a note addressed to the Bradys. Peter carried it inside the house and then sat down to open it.

Inside the envelope was a small sheet of note paper with a short message: "IF YOU KNOW WHAT'S GOOD FOR YOU AND DON'T WANT YOUR FAMILY TO BE HURT BAD, YOU'D BETTER LEAVE THIS ISLAND AT ONCE."

CHAPTER NINE

Peter walked outside the house and reread the note, over and over again. Each time as he reread the note, cold chills ran up and down his spine. The mystery was deepening, and it seemed for sure now that the ghost of Red Andrew was after them. The man he'd seen was undoubtedly working for the pirate. He might even be the pirate himself in modern dress, in a kind of disguise.

He froze as he heard a foot crunch gravel behind him. He imagined that a tall, evil-looking person in a pirate costume was behind him, a black patch covering one eye, a wicked sword raised threateningly.

Peter turned slowly—and breathed a sigh of relief.

"Hi," Jan said. "What's that you've got in your hand?"

Peter quickly crumpled the paper in his fist and assumed an innocent look. He didn't want to alarm his sister by telling her what message the note contained.

"What's *what* I've got in my hand?" he asked her.

She wrinkled her nose in mock annoyance, a gesture that caused her glasses to slip. She pushed them back up with her finger.

"That piece of paper you don't want me to see," Jan said. "What is it, a love letter?"

She giggled at that, but the suggestion brought a frown to Peter's face.

"Of course not," he insisted. "If you want to be nosey, here, look at it."

Peter held the crumpled paper between the thumb and forefinger of his right hand, passed his left hand over it, pretending to grasp the paper but actually letting it fall into the palm of his right hand, which he quickly stuffed into his pocket.

It was a trick that sometimes worked, and this time he did it to perfection. Jan's eyes were glued to his closed left hand which supposedly held the note. She held out her own hand as he pretended to drop the paper into it.

Peter laughed at the surprised expression on his sister's face.

"It's in the *other* hand," she accused.

By that time, Peter had taken the other hand from his pocket. He brought it up and showed that it, too, was empty.

"Hey, that's pretty good," Jan exclaimed. "How'd you do that?"

Peter assumed a mysterious look. "Can't tell

you. Professional secret. If I told you I'd be kicked out of the Magician's Union."

Jan pouted. "You're not a member of any Magician's Union."

"Well, I might be some day," Peter retorted, "and I want to have a clean record."

He was pleased at how well he'd handled the situation, and he could hardly wait for Greg to come back so he could tell him about it. Jan was so fascinated by the trick, she'd forgotten her desire to know what was written on the piece of paper.

The thought of that brought the frown back to Peter's face. If the note were true, it was serious business. If not the pirate ghosts, at least *somebody* was anxious to scare them.

Unless—the thought suddenly occurred to him —it was a practical joke that Jan was pulling. He dismissed that notion as soon as he thought of it. No, it was not in Jan's handwriting, he was sure of that.

Jan's face showed signs of deep thought. "By the way," she began, "you never did tell me——"

"I wish Mom and Dad would get back," he interrupted, realizing she had remembered about the note. "I'm hungry."

"They should be back pretty soon," she said.

As she opened her mouth to say something else, he said, "Guess I'll go get a cold glass of milk. Want some?"

Jan shook her head. "Not right now. I think I'll go back down to the beach and see what Bobby and Cindy are up to."

Nodding, Peter turned and walked back to the

house before Jan could ask him anything else. The idea of a cold glass of milk was very appealing, so he poured himself one in the kitchen and sipped at it for a moment before returning his attention to the threatening note.

Sitting at the kitchen table, he took the warning message from his pocket and smoothed out the wrinkles. No, it definitely wasn't Jan's handwriting, or anybody's that he recognized. It still might be a practical joke—but whose idea of fun would it be?

Lost in his thoughts, he didn't see or hear Marcia come into the kitchen.

"I thought you were outside," Marcia said.

Peter jumped at the sound of her voice. Then he slumped in relief in his chair as he saw it was his older sister.

Marcia laughed. "Wow, are you jumpy. I'll bet you thought I was a ghost or something. Serves you right for scaring Bobby and Cindy with those bedsheets."

"Well, you shouldn't sneak up on people that way," Peter said irritably. Then: "I'm sorry. I guess I'm just nervous today."

"Don't let all this talk about ghosts bother you, Peter," Marcia said. "That's just kid stuff."

Peter grunted. "You didn't think it was kid stuff when Greg was teasing you in the car." He smiled. "In fact, you looked scared."

Marcia reddened. "You were eavesdropping," she said.

"For Pete's sake," Peter said in his defense, "we were all in the same car."

"Well, I didn't think you'd listen to other

71

people's conversations." She thought a moment. "I hope Bobby and Cindy didn't hear any of it. You know how easily frightened they get." She peered over his shoulder. "What's that you're reading?"

Peter had forgotten about the note. He hesitated for a moment. Marcia was a year and a half older than he was, and even though she was just a girl he knew he could tell her. Besides, he was bursting to tell somebody about it.

"I saw a man snooping around the place," he told her. "I followed him, and he got into a motorboat and went away. Then I found this note."

Marcia sat down at the table and took the note. As she read it silently, her face turned pale. When she looked up, she said slowly, "It's from Red Andrew, I know it is."

"Or maybe Black Tom," Peter said excitedly, warming to the subject. "Maybe he thinks we're related to Red Andrew, and he wants revenge for what our ancestor did to him."

Marcia shivered. "But that's silly," she pointed out. "We're not related to Red Andrew. The Roarks were, but not the Bradys."

"How do you know for sure we're not?" Peter persisted. "We might be eighteenth cousins or something. Besides, even if we're not, maybe Black Tom doesn't know that. He might think we're relatives just because we're staying here in this house."

Marcia stared at the paper again. She said, "It's just somebody's idea of a joke, that's all." But she really didn't believe that.

"I didn't tell Jan about it," Peter said in a grown-up manner. "I was afraid she'd be scared."

"You did right, Peter," Marcia told him. "Don't mention it to Bobby and Cindy, either. We'll give the note to Mom and Dad when they get here. They'll know what to do." A frown furrowed her brow. "By the way, where are Bobby and Cindy?"

Peter was relieved to share his secret with someone. He said, "I think they went down to the beach. Jan went down to see what they were doing."

Marcia shook her head. "I told them to stay around the house until Mom and Dad got back." She rose, scraping the kitchen chair on the floor. "I'll make sure they're all right."

"Give me the note back," Peter said. "In case the folks arrive before you get back."

Marcia handed her brother the note, and he proceeded to examine it as carefully as if it were a map showing the location of pirate treasure. The warning disturbed him, but he was also fascinated by the thought that a pirate ghost might actually have left it.

Marcia knew how he felt. It would've been fun spending a vacation here on an island in the Atlantic Ocean even without any ghosts. But the stories they'd heard—even though it frightened them a little—added a sense of adventure to it all.

Trouble was, she thought as she left the house and made her way toward the steps leading to the beach, the stories were one thing and the note was quite another. She could explain away all the talk of ghosts as mere superstition, but the warning message Peter had found was cold, hard fact.

Marcia shivered again and turned her thoughts to other matters. The noonday sun was high in the sky and the ocean sparkled where the sunlight struck it. A gentle cooling breeze moved in from the water, rippling whitecapped waves that frothed and bubbled on the shore.

Marcia paused at the top of the stone steps to look around. Off to one side she could see the big brooding Harker house in the distance, like an inkblot against the clear blue sky. Her eyes roamed the hills and trees, then swept along the white sandy beach. The tiny figure of a girl appeared from behind a clump of rocks, and sunlight glinted from her glasses. Marcia recognized the girl as her sister Jan, but she was perplexed when she saw no sign of either Bobby or Cindy —or of the shaggy dog they'd christened Friday.

She turned her glance up along the coast in the opposite direction, toward Black Tom's Cove, but there were no signs of the youngsters there, either.

"Well," Marcia sighed, "I'll just have to find those two explorers before Mom and Dad get back."

She started down the stone steps. The cool breeze blew her hair as she descended toward the figure of Jan who was now squatting along the shoreline intently examining seashells. As the older girl approached, Jan picked up one of the shells and held it to her ear. Seeing Marcia, the girl motioned for her to be quiet.

Marcia paused, but finally said, "What on earth are you doing?"

Jan kept the shell to her ear. She said, "Somebody told me you could hear the ocean if you held one of these to your ear."

Marcia laughed. "You don't need one of those, silly. The ocean's just a couple of feet from you. You can't help hearing it."

Jan took the seashell from her ear, listened to the tiny waves lapping at the shore near her, and she giggled. "You know something, Marcia, you're right. But the shell is pretty anyway. I'm going to keep it."

"Have you seen Bobby and Cindy?" Marcia wanted to know.

Jan shook her head. "I thought they might've gone back to the house."

"Well, they didn't," Marcia said, "and I'm worried."

Marcia's pretty face showed her concern. She really made the youngsters toe the mark, and they sometimes referred to her as a mother hen, but all knew it was out of genuine concern for them.

"I hope they didn't go over to the Harker house," Marcia added. "I told them not to."

"I don't think they'd do that," Jan said certainly. "They'd be too scared. Besides, there's a big barbed wire fence all around the place."

Marcia's frown grew. "Have you seen Friday the dog?"

"Nope," Jan said with a shake of her head. "I haven't even heard him bark."

"Well," Marcia said determinedly, "we'd better find those two kids before Mom and Dad get back, or else———"

The sound of the station wagon horn up at the house interrupted her.

"Oh, oh," Jan said. "Too late. Don't worry, Bobby and Cindy can take care of themselves. Besides, there aren't really any ghosts or pirates around here, are there?"

"No, of course not," Marcia said, "but there was that note Peter found———"

Marcia realized suddenly she'd said more than she should. Immediately, Jan seized on her words.

"Note?" the younger girl questioned. "Peter found a note?" Her eyes widened in remembrance. "So that was the piece of paper he tried to keep away from me. What did the note say?"

Marcia shook her head impatiently. "We've got to tell Mom and Dad we can't find Cindy and Bobby. Come on."

She started up the stone steps, with Jan close at her heels.

Jan said reassuringly, "Don't worry, Marcia. They're all right. Remember the time they got lost in the Grand Canyon? They just wander off without realizing it, but they're okay."

Marcia paused to squeeze her younger sister's hand and smile. "Of course they are," she said.

Even so, she wished she could be sure of that.

CHAPTER TEN

"I don't like it," Mike Brady said. "I don't like this at all."

As soon as the station wagon pulled up before the house, Peter had run out with the note to show his father. They stood now outside the car, waiting for Marcia and Jan to join them from the beach.

"Maybe it's just somebody's idea of a practical joke," his wife Carol suggested.

"Some joke!" Alice muttered. "If I had any wits left, I'd be scared clean out of them by this time."

"I don't suppose," Greg said to Peter, "that you and Jan made up this note to stir up some excitement?"

Peter bristled. "Of course not. It happened just like I told you."

"Hey, take it easy you two," their father said. "If Peter says he had nothing to do with this, I believe him. One thing I don't want is for everybody to panic. Your mother might be right. This could be just a joke being played on us."

"Sure," Greg chimed in. "I wouldn't put it past some of the townspeople to do something like this—just for us tourists."

Mike said, "Are you sure the man in the motorboat was the same one you saw looking in your window?"

Peter nodded. "I'm positive, Dad."

"He's probably the one who left the note," Carol said.

"Yes," her husband said, "but why?"

"It could still be a practical joke," she said.

"I hope you're right," Mike said. "Just to be on the safe side, though, I'm going to call the police and tell them about this."

Marcia and Jan came rushing up, out of breath.

"Hi," Marcia said. "I suppose Peter told you."

Greg said, "He told us."

"We've looked all over the place," Jan said, "but we can't find them."

Mike paused. "Can't find who?"

"Bobby and Cindy," Jan said, puzzled. "I thought you knew——"

"Bobby and Cindy are gone?" Carol said, her voice rising.

"I just told them about the note," Peter said. "I figured you'd find Bobby and Cindy down at the beach."

"They said they were just going to look around," Marcia said. "They took Friday with them, but I didn't see the dog either."

Carol gripped her husband's arm. "Mike, I'm

78

worried," she said. "If that terrible man in the motorboat——"

"Now don't even think that," Mike told her. "You know how the kids like to explore. They were probably having such a great time looking for buried pirate treasure they lost their way. They'll bump into somebody who'll either head them in the right direction or phone us."

"Sure," Alice chimed in. "Those little chow hounds'll come running just as soon as they smell dinner cooking."

Mike put a consoling arm around Carol. "Alice is right. Now don't worry." He forced a grin. "Right at this very minute they're probably sitting someplace a few hundred yards away but out of our sight, playing in the sand."

"Sure," Greg put in confidently. "After all, this isn't an endless desert in the middle of nowhere."

Carol smiled slowly. "I guess I worry about them more than I should. But I still think of them as my babies."

"Better not let Bobby or Cindy hear you say that," Peter warned. "You know how they hate to be called that."

"You're *all* my babies," his mother said, "no matter how old and grown up you are."

"Okay, let's get organized," Mike said. To Carol: "You help Alice unload the wagon, while the kids help me track down our wandering pair."

The kids gathered around their father, awaiting his orders. They were all concerned about their younger brother and sister and eager to help.

"We'll have to split up," Mike Brady told them. "Jan, you continue along the beach in the direction you were heading. Peter, you go the opposite way. But both of you stay by the shore so you can follow your way back. I don't want any more of you lost, understand?"

The children nodded.

"And keep yelling for Bobby and Cindy," he went on. "They may be out of sight but within the range of your voices."

Peter and Jan walked swiftly toward the stone steps that would take them down to the beach.

"Marcia, you go over the fields in that direction," he instructed, pointing. "They might be playing in those clumps of trees or in the fields behind them."

"Okay, Dad," Marcia said. "If they're there, I'll find them."

She started off.

"I'll head up toward the Harker place," Greg volunteered.

"Right. But don't go onto his property. From what I've heard of the man, Jonathan Harker doesn't welcome strangers."

"I'll be careful, Dad," Greg promised, and trotted off.

Mike watched his oldest son for a moment, then turned and looked down along the beach at Jan and Peter working their way in opposite directions along the shoreline. He could hear their calls of "Cindy" and "Bobby" drift up to him on the cool ocean breeze. Marcia was nearly lost to sight behind a clump of trees in the distance.

A trace of a smile touched Mike's lips. They were a great bunch of kids, and he was mighty proud of them. Suddenly he noticed Alice standing beside him.

"I should've made you all some fast sandwiches," Alice said.

"That's okay," Mike told her. "The search will build up our appetites. We'll all eat together when Bobby and Cindy come back."

Alice and Carol were finishing putting away the groceries when Mike made the phone call to the sheriff's office in town. He told the officer about the note that had been left warning them away from the island, and the policeman said it was probably a practical joke, though most of the inhabitants of the island didn't go in for that sort of thing. He took down the descriptions of Bobby and Cindy and promised to do some nosing around to see if anyone had seen the children.

When he hung up, Carol said, "Let me help you look for them. Alice can stay here and answer the phone in case the police call back."

"That's right," Alice said brightly. "Meanwhile, I'll make some of my famous salad and sandwiches. The kids'll be starving by the time they get back here."

"Okay, come on," Mike agreed. "We'll take the station wagon down the road and see if we can spot them."

His tone was confident, reassuring. They got into the car and drove slowly down the road, looking to one side and another, occasionally leaning out the window to call "Bobby! . . .

Cindy!" There was no doubt in Carol's mind that they would find the children safe and sound, despite the warning note. She was always concerned about the health and welfare of her children, all of them, but especially so of the younger ones who often thought they were bigger and more adult than they really were.

"When those two get home," Carol said determinedly, "I'm going to give them a tongue lashing they won't forget."

Her husband grinned. "No, you won't. You'll be so busy kissing and hugging them you won't have time for it. You're an old softie, lady."

"That makes two of us," Carol said softly.

Mike slowed the car as he stared through the windshield. "There's a kid on a bike heading in our direction."

"It looks like that Adams boy, the one who lives with his mother at the Harker place," Carol said.

Mike braked the car. "I'll ask him if he saw either of the kids."

As he approached, the boy on the bicycle kept darting glances at the Bradys, as though he were afraid of them.

Mike leaned out the window. "John? Can I speak to you for a moment, please?"

John gulped and nodded. He eased his bike closer to the stopped station wagon.

"You remember me," Mike went on. "Mr. Brady. My family and I are staying in the Arnold place."

The boy nodded.

"I was wondering if you'd seen two of my

children," Mike said, and he went on to describe them.

The boy shook his head no.

"Well, if you see them," Carol put in, "will you let us know?"

John Adams shook his head yes, turned his bicycle, and headed back down the road.

"You can't accuse that youngster of being very talkative," Mike said, watching the boy disappear in his rearview mirror.

"He's very shy," Carol said. "He and his sister should be around kids more."

Mike started up the car once again. He said, "We'll invite them both over for some of Alice's home cooking—after we find Cindy and Bobby."

They continued on up the curving road, moving past open fields, slowing near clumps of trees to call out the names of their children. A half hour later they arrived back in town, where they went to the sheriff's office to see if any word had come in on the pair. Sheriff O'Riley, a red-headed man in his mid-forties, said none had.

"But don't worry," he told them. "There's hardly any place on the island a couple of kids can go without being found." He thought a moment. "Unless they went into the caves."

"The caves?" Mike and Carol echoed together.

"There are quite a few caves in this area," the lawman explained, "many of them connected underground. Some of them are very near the shore so the entrances are covered with water during high tide. Some of the ones on land we've closed up to keep kids out of them, but we haven't gotten all of them."

"Oh, Mike!" Carol's face was white. "I hope Cindy and Bobby didn't go in any of them."

"Actually, they're not dangerous particularly," the sheriff assured her. "Most times the kids can find their way right back out if they go inside. Anyway, I sent my deputy out to look over some of them. What I'm bothered about is that note you received. Mind if I see it?"

Mike took the sheet of paper from his pocket and handed it to the lawman, who studied it silently for a moment. "Except for old man Harker, most of the folks around here are friendly and hospitable once you get to know them. I don't know who'd do something like this, even as a joke."

Mike hesitated. *"Could* it have been Harker?"

The sheriff shrugged. "I honestly don't think so. He's a grumpy old coot, but as far as I can tell he doesn't go out of his way to make trouble—unless you get on his property. For the most part, he just stays up there in that big house of his since his wife died, and nobody sees hide nor hair of him—except his housekeeper, Maude Adams, and those kids of hers."

"Mind if I use your phone, sheriff?" Mike asked. Sheriff O'Riley nudged the phone on his desk. "Be my guest."

Mike rang up the Arnold cottage and waited while it rang. Alice answered. "Alice, this is Mr. Brady. Any word from the kids?" He listened for a moment, then said good-bye and hung up.

Carol tensed forward. "Anything?"

Mike shook his head. "Jan followed the shoreline as far as she could, then had to turn back. She didn't find them. What puzzles me is why none of us hear the dog barking."

Carol tugged impatiently at Mike's sleeve. "Let's keep looking."

The sheriff got up and came around his desk. "For all the years I've been sheriff kids have been playing on this island—and nothing bad has happened to any of them yet."

"We really appreciate your help, sheriff," Mike told him. "Let us know if your deputy comes up with anything."

"Will do," Sheriff O'Riley promised. "Just don't worry. Those two kids of yours'll be fine."

Mike and Carol went out to the station wagon. Mike shielded his eyes to gauge the distance the overhead sun was from the horizon.

"Now what?" Carol wanted to know.

"We keep looking," Mike said.

They started the car and drove on up the road, back toward the Arnold house.

CHAPTER ELEVEN

In the darkness of the cave, Cindy sat down on a large flat rock and began to cry.

Bobby paused and said, "Hey, what are you doing?"

"I—I'm resting," she said.

"You are not. You're crying."

"I'm not crying."

"Yes, you are—I can hear you."

"Well, I'm tired, and I'm hungry," Cindy said, "and girls are supposed to cry."

Bobby grunted. "Babies cry, too."

"Don't call me a baby!"

"Well, then, stop crying. You're just scared of the dark—and maybe of the pirate ghosts in the cave here."

Cindy was fearfully silent for a moment. She darted her eyes around but could not see through the darkness. She said finally, "Aren't you scared of the ghosts?"

"Me? Of course not. What's that you're sitting on?"

Cindy reached down to feel the flat, hard surface. "A big rock, I think."

Bobby was glad the darkness concealed his grin. He said, "How do you know it's not the skull of some dead pirate?"

With a shriek, Cindy leaped up. Then she blushed as she heard her brother's laugh. She clenched her fists. "Oh, you! You're mean," she said.

"And you're a scaredy cat," Bobby said. "Why I wouldn't be afraid if a big old ghost came at me right now——"

His words were interrupted by a swift padding of feet, and he was bowled over onto the hard cave floor by a furry body that struck into him.

"Help!" Bobby yelled. "Help, one of the pirate's is after me."

"Woof!" the "pirate" said in the darkness, and Bobby felt a dog's tongue lick his face.

Cindy reached out and felt the dog's furry body. "It's only Friday. He's come back."

Bobby sat up and pushed the big dog from him. "A fine time for it—now that he's got us lost." He'd been trying to keep up his own spirits by kidding about their predicament. The truth was, he himself was scared of the dark and of the possibilities that the ghosts of Red Andrew and Black Tom might really be wandering around in these caves to protect their treasure.

Cindy giggled. "You were scared, too. Go on, admit it."

"Well, maybe a little bit," Bobby said slowly, "but who wouldn't be with a big dog leaping at you in the dark."

87

"I wish we'd never come into this awful place," Cindy said. "I'll bet the others are having lunch right now." She smacked her lips. "I'd give anything for some of Alice's cooking."

Bobby reached into his pocket and pulled out a mashed, partly melted candy bar. "Would you settle for half a candy bar?" he asked her.

"You've got a candy bar?" Cindy exclaimed. "What kind?"

"For goodness sake, what difference does it make what kind? Here we are lost and in danger of starving to death, and you get fussy."

"Well," Cindy said, "I don't like the kind with nuts in it. They get in my teeth."

Bobby sighed and broke the candy bar in half and handed one piece to her. "It doesn't have nuts in it," he assured her.

He sat down on the rock beside her, and they ate silently. He said, "I sure wish I had a flashlight."

"Me, too. I don't like the dark. I wonder if Mom and Dad are out looking for us."

"I'll bet they are," Bobby said.

Cindy hesitated. "I guess they'll punish us for getting ourselves lost again."

"Well, we didn't really get ourselves lost," Bobby said. "It was Friday that got us lost. We couldn't let him stay in the cave all by himself, could we?"

"He's been on Mystery Island longer than we have," Cindy pointed out. "He probably knows his way out of this terrible place."

"Say, that's right," Bobby said with sudden

enthusiasm. "I've got a great idea. Let's see if I still have that kite string in my pocket."

As he fished in his pocket for the string, Cindy said, "Why do you carry kite string in your pocket?"

Bobby shrugged. "You never know when it might come in handy." He pushed aside the pocket knife, the marbles, colored rocks he'd found, and drew forth the tangled string. "Ah, here it is."

"What are you going to do?"

"Tie one end of the string around Friday's neck," he said, fumbling in the dark with the restless dog, "like this. Okay, Cindy, hold my hand."

He helped his sister up, and to the dog he said, "All right, Friday, lead us out of here. Go on, boy, go home."

The dog barked twice and started off through the darkness. The string stretched taut.

"Hey," Bobby yelled, "not so fast."

The string broke, but the dog kept on going. The children could hear his barks echoing in the distance.

"Oh no," Cindy moaned. "We'll never find our way out now."

"Sure we will," Bobby said. "Listen, I'm the man in charge here. Friday's bark came from up ahead. We'll go in that direction."

Bobby was well pleased with the sound of authority his voice made in the darkness. The truth was, he was just as scared as his sister, but he was unwilling to show it.

"Anyway," Cindy said, "it was a good idea, Bobby. About the string, I mean."

"Yeah, thanks," Bobby said.

He held onto his sister's hand and made his way through the darkness, groping along the rough rock wall with his free hand, moving slowly in the direction of Friday's barks which were getting more and more distant. When they found their way back to the cave entrance, what an adventure he'd have to tell the guys back at school about. Even before that, he'd brag to Greg and the others in his own family about how brave and resourceful he'd been.

He gulped and thought: *That is, if we get out of the cave.* He thought of all the stories he'd heard about pirates and ghosts. If any existed on the island, it seemed a safe bet they'd be lurking under the ground in the damp tunnels. He kept trying to fight down the notion that at any instant a ghost would appear—maybe a whole shipload of them, dead pirates intent upon revenge for the two youngsters trespassing on their graves.

Bobby shivered and hoped Cindy didn't notice. He was sure she didn't, because she was doing some shuddering of her own.

"Bobby?" she said suddenly.

He paused and turned to face her. He could barely make out her face, but at first this thought didn't register.

"What is it?" he asked her.

"It's getting lighter," she said. "I can see you."

Bobby stared at her. It was true. He hadn't been able to see her face a moment before. He said enthusiastically, "We must be getting near the entrance to the cave." He peered through the gloom to a point just ahead where the light seemed brighter. "It's probably just around that corner up there. We'll be out in the open again. We'll make it back to the cottage just in time for lunch."

"Let's hurry," Cindy said eagerly.

They hurried.

"Boy," Bobby said, "I'll bet the others were worried about us."

"Do you suppose they'll punish us for getting lost?" Cindy wondered again worriedly.

"Naw," Bobby said, "they'll be too glad to see us for that. C'mon, we're almost there."

He rounded the corner to where the light was brightest and paused, pulling Cindy around beside him. He stared wordlessly at the sight before them. His hopes fell.

"We're not out of the caves at all," Cindy said, voicing their disappointment. Tears of frustration welled in her eyes. "We're lost more than ever!"

CHAPTER TWELVE

Greg Brady hiked up the hill overlooking the ocean. Pausing, he glanced at his wristwatch—only a little past one o'clock. That was a break. Another time when Bobby and Cindy had gotten themselves lost, it was almost dark, so the searchers had to go at it during the night. In the afternoon, with the sun shining, it seemed impossible that anyone could stay lost for very long.

Then he thought about the note that had been left at the Arnold cottage warning them to leave. At first all this talk about ghosts and pirate treasure had been fun. It was a new adventure for them to look forward to, and to experience. But the youngsters' disappearance and the warning message put things in a different light.

Determined, Greg cupped his hands about his mouth and shouted: "Bobby! . . . Cindy!"

He could almost hear the wind take his voice and bounce it along the sides of the cliff. He turned in another direction and repeated the call, then waited, hoping for an answering cry.

Nothing. Only the whispering sigh of the wind and the distant rustle of the restless surf. Greg turned inland, heading in the direction of the Harker house. His father had warned him away from the place, and of course Greg had no intention of setting foot on the old man's property —unless, of course, he were invited, which didn't seem very likely.

His thoughts turned to young Sybil Adams, the housekeeper's daughter, and he remembered their brief conversation in the store in town. Sybil was a pretty girl, with long dark hair and an expressive face. It was a shame she was so shy. If some understanding person were to help her out of her shell, she'd probably have a good personality. Her figure certainly seemed strong and athletic enough. Perhaps before the vacation was over, he'd invite her for a swim in the ocean.

Greg slowed, finding himself in an open area surrounded by trees. Once again he called: "Cindy! . . . Bobby!" to no avail. On impulse, he tried whistling, thinking perhaps Friday would hear and come running to him. In the movies the dog would then lead the rescuers to the place where the missing persons were. Except Friday neither showed up nor barked to indicate he'd heard.

"Maybe it's just as well," Greg said. "Friday's a big lovable bundle of fur, but he didn't seem especially bright to me."

Greg moved on, passing through a small forest of tall green trees. When he came out into a

clearing, a barbed wire fence confronted him—
the unmistakable sign that he'd reached the edge
of the Harker property. He moved along the
fence, heading inland some more, occasionally
pausing to yell out the name of the children. A
moment later, he saw a tiny figure ahead of him
on the inside of the fence. His heart raced, and
for a moment he thought it was one of the children. But no, it was Sybil kneeling beside a small
mound of earth on which she'd placed a tiny
flower.

Greg walked up to the fence beside her and
said, "Hi."

She looked up, startled.

"I'm sorry, I didn't mean to scare you," Greg
apologized.

She smiled and her eyes seemed to sparkle.
"You just surprised me," she said, rising. "I didn't
expect you to be anyplace around here."

"I'm looking for my younger brother and sister," he explained. "They wandered off and got
lost."

Sybil nodded, then lowered her eyes shyly. She
seemed to want to say something, but was hesi-
tant to do so. "I was just putting flowers on
Spooky's grave," she said.

"Spooky?"

"My kitten," she said. "I called him that because he was all black and he liked to sneak
up on me in the dark." She laughed at the pleas-
ant memory, and Greg found himself laughing
with her. She sobered and said, "I suppose you
think that's silly."

"No, of course not," he assured her quickly.

"I think that's very nice," he added, meaning it.

Their eyes met, locked. Greg hadn't realized before how richly brown her eyes were, how deep they seemed, and he knew it was time to change the subject and get back to the business at hand —which was locating Bobby and Cindy.

"Have you seen my brother or sister around here?" Greg asked her. He gave her a brief description of the youngsters.

Sybil shook her head. "I'd notice if any strangers came around here. We don't have many visitors." She looked sad. "As a matter of fact, we don't have *any* visitors. Mr. Harker wants to be left alone."

"From what I hear, that's putting it mildly," Greg grunted. He glanced over the fence at the rolling hills of the estate and wondered if Bobby and Cindy might have crawled under the barbed wire—or maybe unwittingly gone through a break in the fence—and were someplace on the Harker grounds.

"Sybil," he said softly, "may I come over the fence to look for my brother and sister?"

The young girl suddenly looked frightened. She backed away, shaking her head. "No, you can't, Greg. You mustn't. Mr. Harker said——"

"Then let *me* talk to Mr. Harker," Greg insisted. "I'll ask his permission to look around."

Sybil didn't answer. She wanted to let him in, he could tell that, but she was frightened of the old man who was her mother's employer. Her face softened as she moved closer to the fence.

"I—I'd like to, Greg," she said in a small voice, "I'd really like to help you, but you don't know

95

how awful Mr. Harker can be when he's angry. I'm sure he's bitter because his wife left him many years ago, and he doesn't want to see anybody else happy." She hesitated. "He even resented my having Spooky. In fact, I even think he——"

She couldn't go on, but Greg mentally completed her meaning. Sybil suspected that old man Harker had something to do with her kitten's death. He clenched his fists angrily. Jonathan Harker could learn a lot about being a human being.

Then Greg relaxed. There was no sense in being up-tight about it. The safety of Bobby and Cindy were uppermost in his mind. Impulsively, he took Sybil's hand, and the girl flinched and blushed shyly.

"Please, Sybil," he said. "Bobby and Cindy have been gone for hours. We've searched everywhere—except here. Let me talk to Mr. Harker."

The dark-haired girl hesitated once more, then nodded. Greg smiled and had a brief wild impulse to throw his arms around her in gratitude. But he knew that would only embarrass both of them. Besides, he thought wrily, the barbed wire was in the way.

Greg crawled between the two upper strands of wire with Sybil helping to hold the topmost wire from his back.

She said, "Follow me," and led the way up toward the big dark house on the hill. The fields of the estate were lush and green, with clumps of trees. Set apart from the house was a tiny cottage.

"That's where I live," Sybil told him, "with my mother and brother."

"He doesn't allow you in the house either?" Greg said wonderingly.

She shook her head. "Not me or my brother, John. In fact, he won't let my mother in there at night. Not that she wants to go in, because of all the strange things going on."

"What strange things?"

"Moaning noises," Sybil said with a shiver, "and lights flashing on and off."

"Pirate ghosts again," Greg grinned.

"A lot of people around here take it seriously," she reminded him.

"I know," he smiled. "I wouldn't put it past Mr. Harker to've started these rumors himself just to keep people away."

They were silent for a moment as they approached the big, brooding, two-story house. Greg felt a knot of apprehension tie itself in his stomach. All the things he'd heard about old Jonathan Harker had made the man seem as bad as Red Andrew or Black Tom. But he knew it was wrong to judge people purely on what others said, so he decided to reserve judgment.

He didn't have to reserve it for long. They walked up the creaky wooden steps and were approaching the front entrance when the big door suddenly flew open and Jonathan Harker himself stood in the doorway. He was a tall, angular man with a hard, wrinkled face that looked as if it had been chopped out of stone, and a mass of white hair. His eyes blazed angrily and his big body trembled.

"What are you doing here?" he demanded of Greg in a hoarse voice. "You're trespassing, young man, and I could have you arrested, you know that!"

"I just want to talk to you, sir," Greg said quietly. "I'm——"

"One of the Brady family that moved into the Arnold place," the old man finished it for him. "Well, just because you're living there temporarily doesn't mean you have the right to snoop around someone else's property!"

"He wasn't snooping, Mr. Harker," Sybil said. "His brother and sister are lost, and he thought——"

Harker grunted. "Well, they're not here. Look someplace else." He glared at Sybil. "As for you, young lady, I suppose you're the one who brought this intruder here. I intend to have a talk with your mother about this!"

"I have to find my brother and sister, Mr. Harker," Greg insisted. "May I search the grounds?"

"You may not!" the old man barked, starting to close the door. "Now, get off my property immediately or I'll call the police!"

"Wait!" Greg said suddenly.

As the old man paused, Greg listened intently. Then he whistled loudly. A moment later a loud barking came from inside the house, getting closer. Jonathan Harker turned suddenly surprise etching his face, as a shaggy white dog came bounding past him to leap happily all over Greg.

"How did that dog get in my house?" Harker demanded angrily. He glared at Sybil. "You've got a lot to answer for, young lady!"

Harker slammed the door shut.

Sybil turned to Greg. She said, "That's funny. Mr. Harker hates animals." She bent to pet Friday, who was wagging his tail happily and licking their faces. "I wonder how the dog got inside the house."

"I don't know," Greg said, "but I do know that the dog was with Cindy and Bobby before they disappeared."

Sybil gasped. "You don't suppose they're in the house with Mr. Harker?"

"Maybe," the boy mused. "But Mr. Harker was surprised to see Friday. I honestly think he didn't know the dog was in the house."

"Friday?" Sybil said.

"That's what we call him," Greg explained with a grin. "Because it was Friday when we discovered him here on this island."

"I see," Sybil giggled. "Like in Robinson Crusoe."

Greg nodded. "One thing is sure. If the dog is here, then Bobby and Cindy must be, too."

Greg moved down the steps and across the grass, with Sybil beside him and Friday close at their heels. He paused, hands on his hips, and surveyed the rolling hills and patches of trees.

"What are you going to do, Greg?" Sybil asked him.

"Tell my father," Greg decided. "He'll know what to do. I wish I could look around here, though. They might be just over that hill." On impulse, he raised his voice and shouted, "Cindy! . . . Bobby!"

Sybil glanced nervously back at the big house.

In the front window the curtains parted, and she could see the angry face of Jonathan Harker glaring at them.

"You'd better leave," she suggested. "I'll look around for your brother and sister."

Greg grinned and gripped her hand. He didn't realize how his touch embarrassed her until the color filled her cheeks. He released her and moved toward the fence.

"Be careful, Sybil," he said. "Come on, Friday, let's go."

The dog was eager to go with him. Though they hadn't found the missing youngsters yet, Greg felt sure they would—and very soon. It was a good feeling.

CHAPTER THIRTEEN

"Where are we?" Cindy wanted to know.

They had just emerged from the dark tunnel into a big room that seemed part cavern and part basement. Some of the walls were the natural stone of the mountain, while others were obviously man-made.

"I don't know," Bobby breathed, staring in awe at their discovery. His gaze fell upon several old-looking trunks near one wall, and his heart leaped "I think this is where the pirates leave their treasure."

"Pirates!" Cindy exclaimed. "Bobby, let's get out of here, I'm scared."

Girls! Bobby thought. What problems they are. "You want to go back into the caves and get lost in the dark?"

She shook her head. She didn't like the dark, she'd been frightened all during the time she and her brother were wandering through the darkness of the caves. Her eyes flitted over the room, and she gasped as she saw something that terrified her.

"What's the matter?" Bobby asked.

Cindy pointed a trembling finger to a spot across the room where opaque plastic sheets had been draped over large objects whose form and purpose she could not make out.

Cindy gulped. "What do you suppose is under those sheets?"

"I don't know," Bobby admitted. "Probably more treasure."

"Or dead pirates!" Cindy wailed.

Despite himself, Bobby shivered. "Will you stop that? Now come on."

He moved forward into the room, which was lighted by several bare bulbs in various corners. Cindy trailed close behind him, not wishing to stray far from her brother. It was all very exciting, but she wished they were back home with their family again.

Cautiously, Bobby skirted the plastic-covered forms for a moment but could detect no movement from beneath them. Holding his breath, he lifted one end of the sheet and peeked underneath.

"What is is?" Cindy was almost too afraid to ask.

Bobby was puzzled. "Machinery," he said. "Looks like a printing press of some kind." He grew thoughtful. "I wonder what pirates would want with a printing press?"

"Maybe it's not pirates at all," Cindy suggested.

"Don't be silly, of course it's pirates," Bobby said. "Who else would build a big room like this at the end of a tunnel. They probably bring in the gold and stuff from the ocean and store it here. Those trunks over there are probably filled with gold coins and jewels from all over the world."

He began to get excited thinking about it. Suppose he and Cindy had actually found the treasure of Mystery Island! The Brandy Bunch would be rich. With his share he could buy Greg that new hot rod he'd been admiring. Marcia could have an electric guitar. There'd be a new car for his father. And——

His dreams were interrupted by Cindy. "Suppose they come back and find us here?"

Bobby blinked, suddenly brought back to reality. "Who?"

"The pirates," she said, and her voice grew high as she added, "or the *ghosts* of the pirates!"

Bobby felt the blood drain from his face, and chills raced up and down his spine. Cindy was right. Pirate ghosts were around to protect the treasure they'd buried. Right at this very instant, they might be lurking in the shadows ready to spring out at them.

He gulped and nervously glanced around the room, expecting to see one or more of the spirits bearing down on them, saber drawn. But there was only Cindy in the room with him.

"Look," she said. "There's a door over there."

He looked. He hadn't noticed before, but in one corner were some stone steps leading up to a massive wooden door.

"That means we can get out," Cindy said excitedly.

Bobby hesitated. "We ought to at least look at the treasure."

"We can come back," Cindy said, pulling at him. "I want to see Mommy and Daddy again."

Bobby wet his lips. He'd been looking forward to opening the treasure chest and seeing the pile of sparkling jewels, but the spookiness of the place was getting to him. Besides, the trunks looked very heavy, and his father and Greg would have to move them. Also, the Brady bunch always shared things. This discovery should be no exception.

"All right," he said.

Together, they scampered up the few steps to the big door and tried the handle. Bobby tugged at it, twisting the handle, but the door refused to budge.

"It's locked," he said mournfully.

"Oh, no," Cindy wailed. "That means we'll have to go back through the caves again."

"Not necessarily," Bobby said. "Friday came this way, and he's not here in this room, so he must have gotten out somehow."

They were quiet for a moment. Then Cindy's eyes widened. She said, "Listen."

They listened. From the tunnel they'd left came sounds of footsteps.

"Pirates!" Bobby said. The word leaped past his lips before he could stop it.

"Or ghosts!" Cindy amended. "What'll we do?"

"We've got to hide," Bobby told her.

"Where?"

Frantically the youngsters looked around the room. "Come on," Bobby said suddenly, and he grabbed his sister's hand and pulled her with him down the stairs and across the room, where they squatted, out of breath, behind the plastic-sheet covered printing press.

Bobby put a finger to his lips to indicate Cindy should not make a sound and the girl nodded. But her heart was beating very fast, and she was sure that the ghost or pirate or whoever it was would hear it.

The sounds in the tunnel got louder. Bobby's fear was overcome by his natural curiousity, so he peeked around the edge of the plastic sheet to view the entrance to the tunnel. The flickering beam of a flashlight played on the wall of the cave, getting larger and brighter as the person neared the end of his journey. He knew he should duck down, but Bobby's attention was riveted to the opening. He had to see who it was heading for them.

Cindy pulled at his sleeve. "Who is it?"

He shook her off. "Sh!"

Bobby felt his heart pounding in his chest. He wanted to know who it was, but he was frightened to find out. Sure, Greg teased them about ghosts, and so did Peter and Jan, but maybe they really did exist. Suppose that was Red Andrew coming down the tunnel, or Black Tom? What would the pirates do if they caught two children in their treasure room? Make them walk the plank, more than likely. Or worse.

As a shadowy figure loomed in the entrance, Bobby caught his breath and held it. The man emerged into the basement, blinking his eyes in the light. Bobby ducked down quickly so the man wouldn't see him.

Cindy whispered, "Who is it?"

Bobby shrugged. "I don't know. It's not a pirate, and not a ghost, either. I've never seen him before."

They fell silent as they heard the man's footsteps move across the room. Bobby raised his head again to peer over the top of the machinery. The man was dressed in slacks and sportshirt. He was very thin, and his face looked cruel and hungry. Black hair was plastered to his head. As Bobby watched, the man pressed a button set into the wall near the door, then walked back into the room, fidgeting. His hawk face twisted nervously. A sound at the door made him turn around.

Bobby ducked down farther, but no so much he couldn't see the door. The lock clicked open, and the door swung open on oiled hinges. A tall, angular man with a hard face that looked like it never smiled and a mass of white hair on his head came into the room and closed the door behind him.

"Mathews!" the white-haired man growled. "I told you never to come through the tunnel in the daytime."

"Nobody saw me, Mr. Harker," Mathews whined, "I'm sure of it."

Jonathan Harker grunted and came down the steps into the room. "So what did you want to see me about?"

The man hesitated, as though afraid to broach

the subject. Finally, he said, "I think we ought to lay low for awhile."

The older man stared at him. "Oh? And why is that, Mathews?"

"It's that new family in the Arnold place," Mathews said.

"The Bradys," Harker smiled. "Their oldest boy came up here to see me today."

Behind the protective plastic sheet, Cindy's eyes widened. "Greg was here," she whispered.

"Sh!" Bobby cautioned her.

"What about them?" Harker was asking.

"I know you told me to scare them off, Mr. Harker," the other man said apologetically, "but it looks like they aren't going to scare easy."

"You'll have to keep trying, then," Harker barked. "With all those kids around, they might find the entrance to the tunnel leading into this basement." His eyes narrowed at a sudden thought. "As a matter of fact———"

He walked quickly to the tunnel entrance and peered into the gloom, then whirled to face Mathews. "That Brady boy was looking for his brother and sister who were lost. Did you hear or see anything suspicious in the caves?"

Mathews shook his head vigorously. "No, nothing."

"Well, I don't like it," Harker growled. He began pacing nervously. "Everything was going smoothly until that family moved here." He paused thoughtfully. "They'll be gone soon. Maybe you're right. Maybe we should lay low until they're gone."

"See, I do come up with good ideas sometimes,

Mr. Harker," Mathews said, pleased with himself.

Harker grunted. It was obvious he didn't think much of his partner's mental capacity. "What bothers me is the dog."

"Dog?"

"The one the Roark's had when they were here—before we scared *them* off. It came through the tunnel and into the house. I came down here and closed and locked the basement door, but the Brady boy saw the dog and got suspicious. If he goes to the police——"

"The police!" Mathews said suddenly. "I forgot to tell you, Mr. Harker. Mr. Brady went to the sheriff."

"What!" Harker exploded.

Mathews nodded. "I saw him in town. But don't worry, he wasn't after us, he was just looking for a couple of kids."

"Is that all?" Jonathan Harker said sarcastically. "And suppose they come here looking for those kids? Suppose they come down here into the basement looking for them and find what we've got hidden here!"

"I never thought of that," Mathews admitted.

"I'm glad one us has some brains," the old man said gruffly. "We've got to get rid of the evidence. We'll put it in sacks and take it back through the tunnel. I suppose your boat is anchored nearby? Good. Come on, then, let's get moving."

The old man walked to the trunks, extracted a key from his pocket, and bent to open the lock nearest him.

Neither Cindy nor Bobby could resist watching.

Terrified though they were, they raised their heads above the machinery to peer at the two men and the treasure chests they were in the process of opening.

Harker fumbled with the lock, which came free and Mathews leaped forward to lift the lid. Cindy couldn't hold back the gasp of surprise at the sight of the treasure inside the trunk.

"It's filled with money!" she exclaimed.

Bobby groaned and pulled her down with him behind the printing press.

"What was that?" Mathews wanted to know.

Harker's laughter was without humor. "We've found the two little birds who flew out of their nest," he said.

He strode quickly around the machinery and, before either of the children could evade him, grabbed each one roughly by the arm and pulled them into the open.

"Don't!" Cindy cried. "You're hurting me."

"Lemme go," Bobby cried. "Lemme go!"

"Now what are we gonna do?" Mathews asked.

Harker's smile was grim. "Like I said, Mathews, we've got to get rid of the evidence!"

CHAPTER FOURTEEN

"That's a pretty serious accusation, Mr. Brady," the sheriff told Mike over the phone. "I hope you know what you're saying."

"Sheriff, the kids've been missing for hours. It's not like them at all," Mike explained. "They were playing with that shaggy dog the Roarks left here—the same dog that my son Greg saw run out of Harker's house."

The sheriff sighed. "All right, Mr. Brady, my deputy and I will take a run out there. But if we don't find anything suspicious old Jonathan Harker will have a good case against you."

"I'll take that chance," Mike said. "But hurry."

He hung up and told the assembled Brady bunch the conversation.

"Oh, Mike," Carol said, "I do want to find those two wonderful kids, but——"

"Now don't you worry, honey," he said, kissing her on the tip of her nose. "This'll turn out fine, believe me."

"Sure it will," Alice chimed in. "With all us Bradys pulling together, we can't lose."

"All *us* Bradys?" Peter said, raising a puzzled eyebrow.

"Why, sure, Peter," Alice said, twisting his cheek, "Brady's my middle name." She turned to go into the kitchen. "I'll get a snack ready for Bobby and Cindy. They'll be pretty hungry when they get home."

Marcia said, "Isn't there anything we can do?"

"Yeah," Jan put in. "I don't like to just sit around."

"I think there is, Dad," Greg said, suddenly appearing in the doorway.

Behind him came Sybil Adams and her brother John. Greg nodded encouragement at the dark-haired girl. He said, "Go on, Sybil, tell them what you told me."

The girl nodded. "There's a cave not too far from here at the foot of the cliff where Mr. Harker's house is. It's covered by bushes, so I don't think the sheriff's deputy knows about it. But my brother and I sometimes play there." She hesitated. "Once we saw a man go in there and an hour later come out carrying a package."

"Did the man see you watching him?" Mike Brady asked.

Sybil shook her head no. "But we got a good look at him. Greg told me about the man who was snooping around here. It might be the same person."

Mike could not keep the enthusiasm from his voice. "Sybil, can you show us the entrance?"

John's face went white. He touched his sister's

arm. "We'll get in trouble," he said in a thin, frightened voice.

"I don't care," Sybil said. "These people are our friends, John. We must help them." Turning to the Brady bunch, she smiled. "Follow me."

Sybil led the way out of the Arnold house and across the field, followed by Mike and Carol, Greg and Marcia, Peter and Jan. John Adams stood in the doorway watching them, undecided. Alice came from the kitchen.

"Well, I'm glad not everyone's deserted me," she said brightly. "Your name's Johnny Adams, isn't it? Well, Johnny, my name's Alice, and I've just made the best apple pie you'll ever eat. How about a cold glass of milk to go with it?"

The young boy stared at her, undecided for a moment. He wet his lips and a trace of a smile curved his mouth. "I—I don't want to put you to any trouble," he said.

"No trouble at all," Alice assured him. "Alice's my name, and food's my game. Just sit right down at the table and I'll bring it in to you."

On the way to the kitchen, Alice paused to look out at the Bradys heading down the path, the girl Sybil leading them with the dog Friday bounding along beside her. Almost to herself, she whispered, "Hurry home, kids." Then she went to cut two slices of apple pie.

They went Indian file down the stone steps to the beach, then picked their way along the shore for a ways before heading inland, up an incline toward a spot on the side of the hill covered with scraggly bushes.

"I don't see any cave," Peter said, squinting his eyes.

"It's there all right," Sybil said. "I hope you remembered to bring flashlights."

"Got 'em right here," Greg said. "All I could find was two of them."

"That should be enough," Mike Brady decided, taking one from his son. "You and I can go in. Maybe you others had better stay here and wait for us."

"Not on your life," Carol said. "They're my kids, too, and I want to see they're safe."

"Yeah, us too," chorused the others.

Mike sighed. "Okay, but let's all stick together. I don't want anybody else lost." To Sybil he said, "You don't have to go with us, Sybil. You've done more than your share."

"I'll go," Sybil said with determination.

She pulled aside some bushes to reveal a dark entrance. Mike went in first, switching on his light. Carol went next, followed by the Brady kids. Greg and Sybil brought up the rear.

Between the combined lights of Greg and his father, the group could see the well-worn pathway leading through the tunnel of caves fairly well. They made their way quickly but cautiously along.

"It seems to be sloping upward," Greg said after a while.

"I noticed that, too," Mike said. "I was wondering if it leads right up to the Harker house. Sybil?"

"I don't know, Mr. Brady," the dark-haired

113

girl said. "My brother John and I never went in this far. We were too afraid."

"You're not afraid now," Marcia pointed out.

Sybil smiled. "That's because I'm with friends." Her glance went to Greg, and she added, "Good friends."

"What happened to Friday?" Peter asked suddenly.

"He went on ahead," Mike told him. "I guess he knows his way through here pretty well."

They went on through the darkness, pausing from time to time when the tunnel split up into two caves, sometimes more.

"A person could really get lost in here without any light," Carol said. "Those poor kids. How frightened they must have been."

Greg and his father played their flashlights on the dirt floor. They could clearly see the footprints Friday had made. Confidently, they followed the clues the dog had left for them.

"That's a smart dog," Peter said admiringly. "Leading us right to the pirates. Can we take him home with us, Dad?"

"We'll see," his father promised. "Now be quiet. I hear something ahead."

Pausing, Mike played the beam of his flashlight along the pathway ahead, where it stopped abruptly and turned left. Cautiously, he edged past the corner and flashed his light into the new area. Mike Brady's groan echoed dismally in the rocky cave.

"Mike, what is it? What's the matter?" Carol asked, easing along beside him.

"*That's* the matter," he told her, pointing with

the beam of his flashlight while the others crowded around to see.

In the twin beams of the two flashlights they saw the dog Friday lying on its side where the tunnel abruptly ended with a solid brick wall. They had referred to the dog as "he," but they were mistaken—a fact made obvious by the litter of six furry puppies crowding around their mother to be fed.

"Friday led us down the wrong tunnel," Mike said.

"Yeah," Greg added. "Now, *we*'re the ones who're lost!"

CHAPTER FIFTEEN

Bobby and Cindy sat huddled on the steps in the basement while Jonathan Harker paced back and forth trying to figure out what to do with them.

"I'm scared," Cindy confided in a hoarse whisper to her brother.

"Don't worry, Cindy," Bobby said, "I'll protect you."

He tried to sound very grown up, but his voice cracked in mid-sentence. The truth was, he was just as scared as she was, but he wasn't going to admit it.

"Besides," he added, "I'll bet Mom and Dad and Greg and the rest of them are on their way here right now."

"Well, I wish they'd hurry," Cindy said impatiently. "I'm hungry."

"I thought you said you were scared."

"Well, I'm both. There's no law that says I can't be scared and hungry at the same time, is there?"

"Hey, you two," Mathews, the hawk-faced man said irritably, "knock off the chatter. Can't you see Mr. Harker's trying to think?"

The youngsters fell silent and stared at the old man who had stopped pacing and was staring thoughtfully at them. Harker shook his head.

"I had a good thing going," he said sadly, "and you two kids have to come along and spoil it for me."

"We're—we're sorry, sir," Bobby said. "We didn't mean to come here. We followed the dog, and we got lost. Let us go, and we won't tell anybody about the pirate treasure."

Harker stared at them, puzzled for a moment. Then he laughed. "Pirate treasure? Is that what you think you've stumbled on here?" He grew thoughtful. "Well, in a way, maybe you're right. Would you two believe that I'm a descendant of Black Tom, the Pirate?"

Cindy nodded and managed to find her voice. "If you say so, sir."

"Well, I do say so, because it's true. I've had fun frightening the wits out of people on Mystery Island. Sometimes it was just for fun. Other times it was because I didn't want them snooping around, finding the tunnel from the ocean to this house, discovering what I've been doing up here all these years."

Harker went near them and wagged a finger under the children's noses. "Well, I'm not going to prison because of you two kids."

Mathews cleared his throat. "We could take them back out the tunnel to the ocean," he suggested.

Harker whirled on him. "What on earth for?"

Mathews seemed surprised by the question. "Well," he said uneasily, "you said we should get rid of the evidence."

"I meant the counterfeiting plates, idiot," Harker barked at him, "and the phony money in those trunks."

Mathews shook his head wildly. "Not me, Mr. Harker. You can do with it whatever you want, but I'm not waiting for the police. I'm getting out of here."

The hawk-faced man whirled and ran up the stairs, brushing past Bobby and Cindy. As he reached the door, it swung open and Sheriff O'Riley and his deputy came in with revolvers drawn, backing him down the steps once more. Behind them was grim-faced Maude Adams, who'd let them into the house.

Jonathan Harker turned toward the tunnel— only to be met by a huge bundle of furry dog that leaped out and bowled him over backward.

"Friday!" Bobby and Cindy shouted in gleeful unison.

They ran to the dog and began hugging and kissing it. Friday wagged her tail happily.

"Bobby! Cindy!"

Mike Brady emerged from the tunnel, with Carol a close second. Both parents hugged the children to them.

"Thank heavens you're both all right," their mother cried.

"Of course we're all right," Cindy said, a little annoyed. "After all, we're not babies, you know."

At dinner that evening, Bobby and Cindy told of their adventures in the cave leading to the Harker house.

"It was so dark," Bobby said breathlessly, "I couldn't see my hand in front of my face."

"Why would you want to see your hand in front of your face?" Peter asked with a straight face.

Jan giggled, and Bobby glared at her. "That's just an expression," Bobby explained. "Like I said, it was darker than anything, and these pirate ghosts were all around us——" He paused dramatically. "But was I scared?"

"Yes, you were scared," Greg said teasingly.

Bobby frowned, opened his mouth, then broke into a grin himself. "Well, maybe a little," he admitted.

His father said, "I'm sure both of you were very brave."

"That's right," their mother said. "And we're all very glad to have you back safe and sound."

Alice bustled in from the kitchen. "Anybody want some more apple pie? How about you, Johnny?"

Sprinkled among the Brady bunch around the table in the Arnold cottage were Maude Adams and her two children, Sybil and John, who had gratefully accepted the Bradys' invitation to dinner.

"No thanks, Alice," John said, shaking his head. "I've eaten so much it's coming out of my ears."

Peter opened his mouth to comment on that,

but Greg interrupted him with, "It's just an expression, Peter," and everyone laughed.

The events of the day had built up a tension in everyone that was now swiftly draining away. Harker and Mathews had been taken into custody by Sheriff O'Riley, who had also taken the printing plates and the counterfeit money.

"I feel sorry for Mr. Harker," Maude Adams said, striking a serious note. "The poor man's wife was ill for a long time, and doctoring her took all his money. I guess rather than sell the old house, he became desperate and did what he did."

"If it hadn't been for good old Friday," Greg put in, "he would've gotten away with it, too."

"Yeah," Alice said. "When we get home, we'll really have a shaggy dog story to tell everyone!"

"When are you leaving?" Sybil asked softly. The question was supposedly directed at everyone, but she couldn't keep her eyes from Greg.

"In a few days," Carol said. "I hope we see a lot of you and John before we have to go back to California."

"Can we take Friday and the pups with us, Dad?" Bobby wanted to know.

His father laughed. "I hardly think we have room for all of them. Besides, the puppies should stay with their mother for a while longer."

"That's right," Cindy said knowingly. "Without their mother, the little puppies might wander away and get lost."

"Maybe Sybil and John would like to keep the dogs," Greg suggested.

"Hey, that's a great idea," John said with more

enthusiasm than he'd shown in a long time. "How about it, Mom?"

Maude Adams smiled. "If you want to."

"We'll name the dog Friday Brady," John said.

"And there are six pups," Sybil said. "We'll name them Bobby, Cindy, Jan, Peter, Marcia, and Greg."

Marcia grinned. "I wonder how she happened to think of those names."

"Maybe because they're really chow hounds," Alice suggested. "You should see them out here in the kitchen."

Everyone got up and trooped out to the kitchen to watch Friday and her own private Brady bunch lying on a blanket Mike and Carol had placed for them in one corner.

"It's a nice night," Greg said to Sybil. "Care to take a walk?"

"I'd love to," the dark-haired girl said.

"Yeah, that's a great idea," Peter said.

"Not you, dummy," his sister Jan said, grabbing her brother's sleeve and holding him. "Can't you see they want to be alone?"

"What for?" Peter wanted to know.

Jan sighed. "Maybe someday I'll explain it to you—when you're older, of course."

Mike glanced at the frowning face of his son Bobby. "What's wrong, Bobby?"

"Nothing," Bobby said, "except I'm sort of sorry there weren't really any pirates or ghosts or treasure chests filled with gold."

"We've found something else here, Bobby," Carol said, "that's better than all the gold and jewels in the world, and far more lasting."

121

"What's that, Mommy?" Cindy asked.

"Finding and helping new friends," Marcia said, smiling at John.

Outside the cottage, Greg and Sybil walked slowly along the path to the stone steps, then paused to look down at the restless Atlantic Ocean, where a ribbon of rippling moonlight played from the full moon hanging high above the horizon. The night was mild, with a light breeze blowing in, and the sky was black velvet sprinkled with the gems of stars.

"When I was very small," Sybil said softly, "I used to lie on my back in the grass and stare up at the stars. It seemed like I was in another world."

"Me, too," Greg confessed. "Sometimes I still do, back home in California. We have the same stars there that you do here."

The dark-haired girl hesitated. "I—I'm going to miss you, Greg. Both Johnny and I have been very lonely, very shy. We never made friends— until now. Until we met the Brady bunch."

"Maybe you can come out to California sometime for a visit," Greg suggested.

"I'd like that. I think I have an aunt out there we could stay with—in Anaheim. Is that anyplace near where you live?"

"Pretty close. I'll drive out and get you," he promised.

Meanwhile, they had two full days left them. The entire group picknicked and hiked and swam and sunbathed. They rented bicycles, and everyone rode all over Mystery Island, exploring the byways.

"I'm very grateful you all came here for a vacation," Maude Adams confided to Mike and Carol. "Sybil and John hardly said two words to anybody before. Now look at them. You can't shut them up."

It was true. The two Adams youngsters were laughing and playing and bubbling over with enthusiasm as much as the Bradys. All they had needed was to be freed from their shells, and the Brady bunch had done that.

As expected, parting was difficult. Despite the danger and excitement, it had been a fun-filled vacation for all of them.

As the ferry took the Bradys toward the mainland, Marcia looked back at the island and shivered. "Imagine how silly we all were to be frightened," she said. "We thought that the ghosts of Black Tom and Red Andrew would be fighting over us."

Mike Brady grinned. "In a sense they were, Marcia." When the kids stared quizzically at him, he continued. "I forgot to tell you. You remember that red-headed sheriff who helped us find Bobby and Cindy?"

"Sure," Peter said. "Sheriff O'Riley."

"Red Andrew's last name was O'Riley," his father said. "And Jonathan Harker was a descendant of Black Tom."

"I see what you mean," Carol said thoughtfully. "Maybe the spirits of the original pirates were in the bodies of their descendants."

They were silent as they leaned on the railing of the ferry and watched the speck of land disappear gradually from their sight, becoming smaller, vaguer, almost unreal. But they knew it was real, all right, and they would think of it often during the next months and years no matter where they were—of the fun they'd had, of the friends they'd made, and of the treasures they'd discovered on Mystery Island.

C'mon and Join
The Official

BRADY BUNCH
Fan Club!

The Only Official Fan Club for TV's Famous Family

And here's what each fabulous fan club kit contains:

★ **FREE RECORD:** Each member of "The Brady Bunch" has a personal message just for you.

★ **ALL NEW BOOK:** Inside story of "The Brady Bunch." Available to members only. Find out what each Brady is like.

★ **AUTOGRAPHED PORTRAITS OF EACH STAR:** Beautiful, never-before-seen photos for your wall, locker, or scrapbook.

★ **COLOR BRADY STICKERS:** Dozens of stickers for your letters, books, and mirrors.

★ **MEMBERSHIP CARD**

★ **AUTOGRAPHED WALLET-SIZE PHOTOS** of every cast member.

★ **EXTRA BONUS——BIRTHDAY GUIDE & FACT SHEET:** Every bit of information you need on each Brady!

SEND YOUR NAME, ADDRESS plus $2.00 to:
Brady Bunch Fan Club, Dept. MI
Drawer L
Hollywood, Calif. 90028

Add 25¢ for postage and handling.

(Outside U.S.A. send $3.00 in international money order.)